JANIE BOLITHO was born in Falmouth, Cornwall. She enjoyed a variety of careers – psychiatric nurse, debt collector, working for a tour operator, a book-maker's clerk – before becoming a full-time writer. She passed away in 2002.

D1003051

By Janie Bolitho

Buried in Cornwall
Killed in Cornwall
Caught Out in Cornwall

a&b

CAUGHT OUT IN CORNWALL

JANIE BOLITHO

Allison & Busby Limited
12 Fitzroy Mews
London W1T 6DW
www.allisonandbusby.com

First published in Great Britain by Allison & Busby in 2003.
This paperback edition published by Allison & Busby in 2012.

A CIP catalogue record for this book is available from
the British Library.

10 9 8 7 6 5 4 3 2 1

ISBN 978-0-7490-1168-0

Typeset in 10.5/15.3 pt
Sabon by Allison & Busby Ltd.

The paper used for this Allison & Busby publication
has been produced from trees that have been legally sourced
from well-managed and credibly certified forests.

Printed and bound by
CPI Group (UK) Ltd, Croydon, CR0 4YY

*Janie Bolitho died from cancer
on the 27th September 2002.
This book is dedicated by her family
to her loyal readers.*

CHAPTER ONE

A small crowd began to gather. One minute, apart from a few distant dog walkers, Rose Trevelyan was alone on Marazion beach; the next about a dozen people had arrived to witness the ensuing drama. As she gazed out to sea with her hands in the pockets of her warm, wool jacket, the wind whipped her hair around her face and sent fine particles of sand skittering across the toes of her boots.

The tide was high, the causeway leading to St Michael's Mount, the home of Lord St Levan, was covered by the broiling water as the wind pushed it further landward. White spume rode along the top of the waves.

It was November and at three p.m. the light was already fading as low, heavy rain clouds were swept across the expanse of the bay. Rose had seen the maroon set off from the yacht which now drifted dangerously. Its mast had snapped. The sails, still partially attached to the boat, dragged heavily in the rough sea. It could not have had an engine unless that, too, had failed.

She had used her mobile phone to alert the coastguards but someone had beaten her to it; someone who may well have seen what had happened before the flare exploded in the sky.

It started to rain. Large spots dimpled the fine white sand. Suddenly rain was sweeping up the beach and stinging the faces of the intrepid onlookers. But it had always been that way in Cornwall. Since the days of smuggling and times when more numerous shipwrecks occurred, whatever the weather, the locals would turn out to help, or if that failed, to plunder if a ship went down.

The lifeboat came into view, its blue and orange colouring a welcome sight. How brave were those men who risked their own lives for somebody else's. But they were never forgotten. Even now the Newlyn Christmas lights were switched off on the 19th of December in memory of the crew of the Penlee lifeboat who lost their lives in an unbelievable feat of bravery. Men; fathers and sons who, on that storm ridden night had refused to give up until every option had been tried, by which time it was too late for them as well as those they had been trying to rescue from the doomed *Union Star*.

Rose understood the cost to their families. She had been devastated when David, her husband, had died from cancer. That was several years ago. More recently had come her mother's death.

A small child, a girl of about four, walked past. She was dark-haired and healthy-looking, although not suitably dressed for the weather for she wore no coat over her jeans and jumper. At first she appeared to be alone. Rose watched with suspicion when a man leant down to speak to her, then relaxed as the child held up its arms and said 'Carry me'. The man picked her up and hurried up the beach towards the car park. The pair of them were soaked.

Squinting, Rose could just make out the line that ran from the lifeboat to the disabled yacht. Visibility was poor; the scene shrouded with rain, but there was movement aboard the yacht.

A woman screamed, then. 'Beth,' she shouted. 'Oh, my God, Beth.'

Rose was confused, not understanding that two dramas were being played out, one at sea, the other on land. A tall young woman turned her head from side to side, frantically searching the beach. She groaned then stumbled amongst the crowd. 'Have you seen my daughter? Have you seen my little girl?' she repeated.

'What does she look like, maid?' an elderly man enquired.

'She's only four. She's got long dark hair and she's wearing jeans.'

Rose frowned. The description fitted the child she had seen, but that child had gone off happily with the man. There must have been a misunderstanding. She approached the woman, who was now crying. Someone was ringing the police. Rose touched her arm. 'I think I saw Beth. She went off with a man. Could it have been her father? She didn't seem at all distressed.'

'No. No, that's impossible. He doesn't know we're here.'

Rose hadn't wanted to give the woman false hope but it was unlikely there were two children fitting that description on the beach at the same time, especially in view of the weather.

Some people would have walked away and left matters to the police. Not Rose. For one thing she was a witness and she knew what the man looked like. Her trained artist's eyes did not miss much. This time her friends could hardly accuse her of interfering; surely they would have done the same?

When the police arrived the lifeboat was towing the yacht away. The second incident had eclipsed the first. How ironic that the crew, now presumably safely aboard the rescue vessel – who had been in far more danger than a child in the relative safety of a West Country beach, in the care of her mother – had been saved, whilst the girl was now missing.

One of the policemen put a blanket around the shoulders of the woman and led her up the beach to where the patrol car was parked. Having given some barely coherent details she was now shivering too much to be able to speak at all.

'Did anyone here see anything that might be relevant?' the second, younger officer asked. Rain glistened on his plastic cape.

Rose swallowed. 'Yes. At least I think I did.' What would Inspector Jack Pearce think when he heard of her involvement? If he heard. Maybe the little girl was safe, sitting in a Marazion cafe with someone who knew her, drying out and getting warm. Jack Pearce was her lover. Well, some of the time. He was never able to understand how her interest in people led her into situations where crime was involved and which sometimes put her in danger. She was aware that she always acted before she thought. But look at today. She had simply come to study the sea because there was a blank canvas waiting to be filled and she needed inspiration. A seascape; she had already decided that, a winter seascape painted in oils. The last two had been done in acrylics. Had the maroon not gone off she would have made some preliminary sketches.

'I'll need to ask you some questions, madam. Can you spare a few minutes?' Rose nodded. The PC spoke into his radio requesting back up.

'Can any of us do anything?' It was the man who had spoken to the distraught woman who asked.

The PC organised them into a rough sort of search party and those who were willing to stay spread out along the beach. There were rocks behind which the child might be hiding. 'Let's get in the dry,' he said to Rose.

She followed him up to the car. The woman was in the back, the blanket clutched tightly to her. Her face was expressionless. Rose gave her name and address. 'The child I saw fits the description but she went off willingly with a man. She asked him to carry her.'

'I see. Can you describe him?'

'Yes. He's about six foot, certainly no less, well-built, he's got dark hair and he was wearing jeans and a sort of parka-style jacket. It had a hood but he wasn't wearing it.'

'Thank you.' The PC had been making notes.

'Does it sound like anyone you know, Sally?' the first officer asked. The woman shook her head. 'Are you married or living with anyone?'

'Neither.'

'And Beth's father? Could it have been him?'

'No. We moved down here about five years ago. He hasn't seen her since she was a baby and he doesn't even know we're here.'

'I see. Does he have any access to Beth?'

'No.' She paused, then decided to be honest. 'Not any more, but that's down to me. I didn't want anything more to do with him and didn't want him to have contact with Beth. We weren't married.'

'Are you certain it couldn't have been him?'

'Yes.'

'All right, we'll get you home now. It's the best place for you to be, there's nothing you can do here.' He turned to Rose. 'Mrs Trevelyan, do you require transport?'

'No thank you, I've got my car.'

'We might need to speak to you again.'

She was aware of that. If the little girl had been abducted she might have to go to court if they arrested the man. She refused to think of whatever else might happen to four-year-old Beth. 'Have you anyone to sit with you?' she asked, knowing that a female officer would be despatched to the house, that Sally would not be alone. But she might like the company of another woman, one who was not in authority.

'It's all right, I'll be fine.' She did not sound as if she would.

'Look, I'll give you my number. If you need anything, just ring me.'

'You're very kind. Thank you.'

Rose unlocked the car, got in and started the engine. It was doubtful that Sally would telephone but Rose was glad she'd made the offer. Cold and tired, she drove back home.

Her house in Newlyn had magnificent views of the bay and an ability to restore her equanimity. It had been her home since her marriage to David all those years ago and she had no intention of moving. It was granite built, like so many properties in the area, and stood at the top of a steep drive. To the left of the drive was the garden and a shed which she had converted to a working area for the summer months. Inside, nothing much had been altered since the day it was built apart from the addition of a modern bathroom and kitchen. She unlocked the kitchen door; she rarely used the one at the front, flicked on the light switch and was immediately grateful for the warmth of the central heating. Filling the kettle, she prayed that Beth was already safely back with her mother. But somehow she doubted it. It was dark now but she never drew the curtains. Impossible to cut off that view. She made coffee and took the mug through to the sitting room. The darker outline of St Michael's Mount was just visible. All along the curve of the coastline lights twinkled. To the left, down in Newlyn Harbour, many fishing boats were safely moored. Trevor's would be one of them. Laura Penfold, Rose's best friend, had said her husband was landing that day, that the storms were due to last for some time. The conditions were not conducive to successful fishing and, besides, it was far too dangerous. She could see the waves splashing against the walls of Penzance promenade even though the tide was now ebbing.

She had not realised how cold and wet she was but, gradually, warmth returned to her limbs. She took off her coat and went back to the kitchen.

Her father was coming for supper; it was time to get it started.

Arthur Forbes had once been a Gloucestershire farmer. When the red tape involved had become too restrictive he had taken early retirement and bought a cottage in the Cotswolds. He and Rose's mother, Evelyn, had been happy there and had made the garden their main hobby. Evelyn had died less than a year ago and almost immediately after her death Arthur had decided to move to Cornwall to be near his daughter, his only living relative. A month previously he had bought a three bedroom house in Penzance, one which Rose considered to be too big for him but she kept her opinion to herself. It was his choice, not hers. How strange it was to have him so near, and to have him alone. She recognised and appreciated the efforts he made not to appear demanding upon her time or hospitality. Fortunately they were both independent people and could survive that way. It had now become a weekly ritual that Arthur would eat with Rose. Now and then they went out for a meal.

Rose smiled. Her staple diet was fish, given to her by Trevor or one or other of the fishermen she knew. There was always plenty, some of which she gave to her father.

She hoped he wouldn't object to it again tonight. Once she had skinned the monkfish and cut strips from its central bone, she prepared the vegetables.

At seven fifteen she heard her father's car in the drive and opened the kitchen door. It was no longer raining but the wind was gusting round the building. However, it had stood there for over a century and could withstand worse weather than this.

'Hello, darling. What a night.'

Rose shut the kitchen door and kissed his cheek. 'Ready for a drink?'

'Yes, please. I'm surprised you haven't got one on the go-'

She laughed. 'You're beginning to sound as bad as Jack Pearce.'

'Well someone needs to keep you in check. What is it?' Her smile had faded. 'Has something happened?' He sat at the kitchen table while Rose got out glasses and poured wine.

'Yes, it was all very strange.' She explained what had taken place on the beach as she tried to piece the events together.

'Have you listened to the news? Maybe they've found her by now.'

It hadn't occurred to her. It was too late for

the local television news but they could listen to Radio Cornwall later. She sat down and decided to lighten the mood. Her father had not yet had time to grieve properly, she did not want to make things harder for him by appearing worried. He looked older and frailer now, although Rose suspected his robustness might well return with time. At least the new house was keeping him busy. Together, they had chosen wallpaper and paint and Arthur spent his days decorating. Rose knew he would need to find other interests once the work was complete. At least he had a garden which needed a lot of work to keep him occupied.

'Seen much of Jack lately?' Arthur tried to sound casual but he desperately hoped that Rose and Jack would get together on a permanent basis. Her many friends shared the same view, as had her mother.

'When neither of us is not too busy.'

Subject closed, he thought. 'And Barry?

'Ah, yes, Barry. To my amazement he's still seeing Jenny.'

'You see, it's never too late to change.' Arthur had known Barry Rowe for almost as long as his daughter had done, over a quarter of a century. To his and Evelyn's surprise, once Rose left art college she had come to Cornwall to study the

Newlyn and St Ives schools of painting. But she had never returned. Within months she had met David Trevelyan and married him within a year. Her marriage had been a happy one, but one without children, which was not for the lack of trying. Naturally her parents had been disappointed but they had come to accept that it wasn't to be. It had been Barry who had introduced Rose to David, who happened to walk into the shop as Rose was delivering some watercolours for Barry to copy and turn into blank greetings cards. She still did this sort of work for him as well as taking photographs, which would be converted into postcards. Barry's business, comprising the Penzance shop and the Camborne print works, was successful. 'You told me he'd smartened himself and his flat up considerably; was this all in aid of Jenny?' her father enquired, mischievously.

'No. Those things happened before. Maybe meeting her was just a natural progression.' Ever since he had met her, Barry had loved Rose but she had always made it clear she had no more to offer than friendship. As far as she was aware there had never been a woman in his life about whom he was serious. Now, at the age of fifty, he had suddenly found one. Rose, expecting to have felt a twinge of jealousy after all his years of devotion, only felt pleasure. She liked Jenny.

The monktail, baked in the oven with fennel and a squeeze of orange juice, was ready. Rose served the meal and they talked of general things as they ate. When the dishes were done they listened to the news. Rose guessed what was coming by the solemnity of the announcer's tone.

'Four-year-old Bethany Jones, who was with her mother on Marazion beach, was seen leaving the beach with a man at around three twenty this afternoon. Bethany is still missing. The police have mounted a full scale search and they have been assisted by volunteers,' the announcer continued before asking for assistance from the public and giving a number to ring if anyone had any information.

Rose sighed. Jack had always told her that the longer a child was missing, the less likely he or she would be found alive. It might have been a judgemental opinion, but from what Rose had seen of Sally Jones it seemed unlikely that she had the sort of money which would attract a kidnapper wishing to demand a ransom. She appeared malnourished and her clothes were threadbare and cheap.

'I'd better go, Rose. Thanks for a lovely meal.

My turn next time. I'm becoming a dab hand at stews and even your mother would be proud of my dumplings. And, look, try not to worry. The police will do all they can to find her.'

But Rose *was* worried. Supposing Beth had been abandoned somewhere, what chance would she have of survival, especially in this weather? 'Ring me tomorrow,' she said as she handed him his coat. It had become a daily ritual since her mother's death. It was reassuring for them both.

She made tea and took it up to bed along with the novel she was reading. However hard she tried she could not get the picture of the pinched, forlorn face of Sally Jones, with her spiky fair hair, out of her mind.

She looked like a victim. Perhaps that was why she had become one.

Rose turned out the bedside lamp and pulled the duvet around her shoulders then lay listening to the storm until she finally fell asleep.

CHAPTER TWO

Although the heating was on and the gas fire in the unused grate was lit, Sally Jones was shivering. Not so Janice Richards, the family liaison officer who had remained with her throughout the night. She was sweating beneath her uniform blouse. Neither of them had slept. For Janice, it was part of the job.

The small lounge of the rented flat smelt stale, the air was thick with cigarette smoke. The previous evening Janice had thoughtfully closed the door of the bedroom where Beth normally slept. There was too much visible evidence of the child who was no longer there. 'Shall we have some more tea?'

Sally nodded. They hadn't drunk half of the cups they had made through the long hours of the night, but it had given them something to do.

On the three occasions that Janice had answered the telephone Sally's hopes had been raised. But there had been no news. Beth had simply disappeared.

'Are you certain her father couldn't have taken her?' Janice asked once more when she returned with the tea.

'Positive. I know he thinks the world of her but he couldn't possibly look after her. Besides, as I said, he doesn't even know where we are.'

Michael Poole, Bern's father, was a sales representative and was therefore on the road all day. There were also occasions when he stayed away overnight. Janice had given his address to the officer in charge. Detective Inspector Jack Pearce was following this up. No matter what Sally believed, it was often a father, a mother or a near relative who snatched a child. The previous year Michael Poole had applied for custody, claiming that Sally was an unfit mother. As he had not seen either the mother or the child for a long time his reasons were unclear. However, Social Services reports proved otherwise.

'What time is your sister arriving?' It was

eight o'clock and barely daylight. Janice pulled back the curtains and lowered the flame on the gas fire. Sally made no objection; she probably hadn't noticed.

'As soon as she's spoken to the children. She said they wouldn't be going to school today.'

Janice nodded. Aged six and five they were old enough to understand what was happening.

Carol, Sally's sister, older by two years, had moved to Marazion after her marriage to John Harte. Janice was aware of this and that the family originated from Looe, on the north coast of Cornwall. John was a mining engineer and he, like so many others, had been forced to find work overseas. From tin mining he had changed to oil. He was extremely well paid but his work kept him away from home for long periods. As he was currently in Saudi, and this had been checked, he was not a suspect. Carol had not stayed overnight even though her children were with her mother. Janice was there and would have slept on the sofa if necessary but Carol could not bring herself to sleep in Beth's room.

The police had interviewed Carol the previous evening. 'Since Sally and Michael split up I've only seen him once,' she had told them. 'He was good enough to deliver something my mother was keeping for me.' Carol thought it highly unlikely that Michael had anything to do with his daughter's disappearance.

The sisters' father was dead but their mother still lived in Looe above the souvenir shop she now owned and ran. She had been devastated when she heard what had happened to her granddaughter, but even when she had stopped crying she could think of no one who would have taken her. She had rung Sally, offering to come down immediately, but Sally had refused the offer. It was obvious to the police who had called on Mrs Jones that there was no child on the premises, either in the shop and storerooms or in the flat above. Permission had been given freely for them to search. Alice Jones was not insulted; she knew it was part of their job.

The telephone rang again. Janice picked up the receiver.

'No go as far as Poole's concerned,' Jack Pearce told her. 'We've kept an eye on him overnight and he didn't leave the house. It's also been confirmed that he kept all yesterday's appointments. They were mostly in the Devon area. There just wasn't time for him to have done it. He got home around seven last night, alone, and left again this morning.'

'I see.' Janice did see but she kept her thoughts to herself. If little Beth was not with one of the family, the most obvious place to start, the chances of finding her soon, or alive, were narrower. The puzzling thing was that if Mrs Trevelyan was telling the truth, and there was no reason to suspect otherwise, and the child had gone willingly, had even held up her arms to be carried, then it strongly suggested that she knew her abductor well. Or else Rose Trevelyan was mistaken, had seen only what she had expected to see, a father picking up his child, not a man snatching an unknown one from a beach. 'What do you want me to do, sir?'

'Say nothing for the moment, there's no point in adding to her distress.'

A little over an hour later Carol Harte arrived. Sally and Janice were sitting in armchairs each side of the fireplace. Wintry sunlight did nothing to cheer the room. Unlike her sister, Carol's hair was its natural reddish brown. Her body was more rounded, but firm. The only thing they had in common was the pallor of their skin. She hugged Sally silently. There were no words to convey what they both felt and anything that could be said had been said the night before when Carol had come over as soon as the police had left. With Tamsin and Lucy at their grandparents' there had been no babysitting arrangements to make. 'Is there any news?' she asked pointlessly because Sally's face had already given her the answer.

'No, nothing. Oh, God, Carol, what am I going to do?' Without warning, tears streamed down her face. It kept happening, it was something over which she had had no control since yesterday afternoon.

'It'll be all right. They'll find her.' Carol hated herself for the platitudes but how could she say anything else – especially when all three women were beginning to doubt this was true?

This time it was Carol who made the coffee. For the moment there seemed nothing else anyone could do.

Detective Inspector Jack Pearce sat at his desk at the police station in Camborne and ran a hand through his thick, dark hair in which the odd streak of grey was beginning to appear. He could not be mistaken for anything but Cornish even before his accent gave him away. His family went back for generations. With a marriage in the distant past and two grown up sons who still came on regular visits, he was a reasonably contented man. If Rose would agree to commit herself to him then he would be totally happy. On the other hand, he was fully aware that the relationship would be tempestuous. They had that effect on one another. Now that Arthur was living in the area he might be able to put some pressure on his daughter. Arthur, he knew, would love to see them married.

A child is missing, I should not be thinking of Rose, he told himself, except her name had come up on the computer as a witness to the incident, apparently the only witness. Trust her, he thought; trust her to bloody well be involved. This time, however, he could hardly accuse her of meddling, she just happened to be in the right place at the right time. Or the wrong place. Pure chance had taken her to the beach at Marazion.

He looked over the information they had so far, which didn't amount to much; the names and addresses of Sally Jones' family, a full description and a photograph of Beth, and Rose's account of what she thought had happened. The photograph had been copied and distributed to all local officers and the press. It had also been transferred to the computer where it was accessible to every officer nationwide. Apart from Rose's quite detailed description of the man; a description which Jack knew would be more accurate than most, there was nothing else to go on. Presumably he had a car but no one in the car park would have looked twice at a man carrying a child and by then any potential witness would probably have been hurrying for shelter.

Apart from the usual rash of nutters claiming to have the child or to know where she was, no definite sightings had been reported. The man could be anywhere by now. But the nutters' stories had to be checked, they could not afford to ignore them.

A local search was continuing. Jack's worst fear was that Beth had been murdered, never to be found, her body hidden in some deserted spot. And there were plenty of those in West Cornwall.

Satisfied that everything possible was being done he left the building and got into his car. He wanted to talk to Rose. The sky had clouded over and it was colder now, more typical of November. Hopefully she would be at home. But Beth, what chance did she have out there in such weather? The best Jack could hope for was that wherever she was she was warm and well fed.

Rose's car was not in the drive. Jack cursed, scribbled a note and shoved it under the back door.

* * *

The sky was a brilliant palette. Streaks of pink and orange were spread over the whole of the bay heralding the sunrise. Rose watched the colours glow then begin to fade as daylight arrived.

After coffee and toast and one of her rationed cigarettes she showered and dressed and dried her hair. It was auburn and wavy, not yet fading, and shoulder length in the style she had worn since her schooldays. As it suited her there was no point in changing it. She was petite with none of the stretch marks of childbearing, although she would have accepted them readily if she had ever become pregnant. At least she had been able to devote herself to David in the years that they had had together.

Up in the loft, which was reached by a flight of wooden stairs hidden behind a pine door, was Rose's office; a tiny darkroom and her sometimes workplace. The light was good, the Velux windows faced north.

There were a couple of invoices to send out for photographic work she had completed, although she took on fewer commissions these days, as she preferred to paint. Now that she had finally got to grips with the computer she had bought earlier in the year, this took very little time. That done, she studied a couple of paintings that were ready for framing before they went on show in Geoff Carter's gallery. They had been an experiment, they were worked in gouache; a way of painting in opaque colours which were ground in water and thickened with gum and honey. Conversely, the paint could be thinned down. She was pleased with the results but still preferred the medium of oils.

After her marriage Rose had continued to paint, mainly with watercolours, and she had taken up photography for which she also had a natural flair. But since David's death her career had really taken off. Somehow she had found the courage to paint boldly, to not be afraid of the oils and her dramatic work sold successfully.

How proud she was to have had two shared exhibitions followed by one solo show.

She swore when the telephone rang. If it were Doreen Clarke she would never get off the line and she was eager to start work. It was the time of day she usually rang; after breakfast and before she went off to one or other of her cleaning jobs.

The phone was on a small table behind the sitting-room door, placed there so that she could see the panorama of Mount's Bay as she spoke. As tempting as it was to let the answering machine take over, Rose hurried down the two flights of stairs. Curiosity usually overcame prudence. Outside, the wind might be blowing strongly, but the sky was the startling shade of blue only seen in Cornwall.

'Is that Mrs Trevelyan?' an unknown female voice asked.

'Yes, it is.'

'You don't know me and I'm sorry to bother you but my name's Carol Harte, I'm Sally Jones' sister.'

'Is there any news?' For a second Rose thought she was ringing to say Beth had been found but her subdued tone suggested otherwise.

'Unfortunately there isn't. I know it's an imposition but Sally wondered if you'd come over and see her. I don't know what she thinks you can do, but I'll go along with anything she wants at the moment.'

How had the woman survived the night? What on earth must she be feeling? 'Of course I'll come. Give me the address and I'll be there as soon as I can.' She wrote down the directions and hung up.

Despite the sun, it was bitterly cold as the wind was blowing from the east. Rose got into the car and, once the engine was warm, drove down the hill into Newlyn where the fish market was already closing. Several men were hosing down the concrete floor of the slightly raised building. There were no fish boxes to be seen. They had already been loaded on lorries and were on their way to their various destinations. A lone blackback gull demolished a fallen fish in one gulp. She turned on to the Promenade where the fierce wind buffeted her small car. The tide was out now, but later, if the wind remained as strong, waves would sweep over the Promenade railings bringing with them stones and seaweed and the possibility of the road being closed.

Carol's directions were easy to follow. Rose soon arrived in Marazion whose name, with a variation of spellings, meant Thursday Market. It was one of the oldest towns in England, having been granted its first charter of incorporation in 1257 by Henry III. Despite its narrow streets she found somewhere to park, an impossible feat in the summer.

Having walked the short distance to the large, detached house with a small garden she rang the bell above the name Jones. The building had been converted into two self-contained flats. A disembodied voice told her to push the door and go up to the first floor.

At the top of the flight of deep stairs a young

woman was waiting for her. It had to be Carol as it certainly was not Sally.

'Thank you so much for coming. She's had no sleep and she's in a terrible state. But who wouldn't be? Come on in.'

Rose followed her into a small hallway and through a door, which led in to the front room where the warmth enveloped her immediately. The furniture was shabby but not unreasonably so. There was an empty photoframe on the sideboard. Rose guessed the police had taken away Beth's picture. The view from the window showed nothing more than the roofs of the houses below.

In an armchair sat a gaunt, hollow-eyed Sally. Beside her were an overflowing ashtray and a vodka bottle with only an inch or so of spirit remaining. Carol took control and introduced Rose to Janice. 'You've met Sally, of course.' She bit her lip. She'd nearly added, *when Beth disappeared.*

Sally tried to stand, but couldn't. 'Thank you for coming,' she said as tears filled her eyes. 'I don't really know why I wanted to see you again. Maybe I imagined I'd feel better talking to the last person to see her before that man took her.'

'Talking often helps.' Rose knew the words

were facile but she had no idea what else to say, and even less idea how to offer the comfort Sally so desperately required. 'I've told the police everything I remember seeing. I just hope it's been helpful.'

'Can you describe the man to me again? I wasn't really taking in very much yesterday.'

Rose did so as she tried to think of anything she might have missed, some small but vital detail that would lead to his identification and restore the child to her mother. She was aware that Janice was taking it all in even though she wasn't taking notes. Perhaps the PC's presence here would mean a second interview with the police would prove unnecessary. However, there was nothing she could add and the description did not fit anyone that Sally knew.

Rose refused the offer of coffee and left after a fruitless half hour. She had been unable to offer Sally any hope. It was Carol who walked with her to the front door. 'I'm glad my sister's moved down here. She needs looking after and Mum's always too busy with the shop. She did offer to come straight down yesterday evening but Sally said no. Sally's life hasn't been easy.' She paused. 'John, that's my husband, and myself, well, we both think she might be an alcoholic but doesn't realise it. You must've noticed the vodka bottle.'

Rose had, but in the same circumstances it was something to which she might have resorted herself. But why was Carol telling her this? I must not get involved, she thought, although for some reason she got the impression that Carol Harte was a manipulative woman and actually wanted her to become involved.

A door to their right opened and an elderly woman stood in its frame. 'Ah, I thought I heard voices,' she said. 'Has Sally had any news?'

'No, I'm afraid not. This is Rose Trevelyan; she's the lady who last saw Beth. Rose, this is Mrs Penhalligon.'

Mrs Penhalligon looked at her sharply in a way which suggested that Rose, herself, might have abducted Beth, but that was not what was going through her mind. 'I know the name. You're an artist, aren't you?'

'Yes.' It always pleased Rose when her name was recognised, although Mrs Penhalligon in her ill-fitting dress, sensible shoes and tightly permed hair did not strike her as someone who would be interested in art. But presumptions are foolish and Rose was proved wrong.

'I've seen some of your work. It's not bad at all.'

'Thank you.' This was more of a compliment than it sounded. The lady in question bore a strong resemblance to Doreen Clarke who, on a first meeting had said something very similar. Now there was no stopping Doreen's hyperbolic praise.

'I'm Norma, by the way, Sally's landlady. I had a big family once but when Harry passed on and the children had all left home I couldn't see the sense in keeping on a large house. But I didn't want to move either. I had a few alterations made and this way I've got the best of both worlds. The extra money comes in handy, too.

'Anyway, it was nice to meet you. Drop in any time if you're over this way. I'm never far away.' Norma Penhalligon shut her door as quickly and as silently as she had opened it.

'Thank you again for coming,' Carol said as she opened the main door for Rose.

'I don't think it did any good but it was no trouble.' Rose walked back to the car, glad of the fresh air after the heat of Sally's front room. It had been a strange visit; there were undercurrents she couldn't quite pinpoint. Even Mrs Penhalligon had seemed to be offering a challenge by way of inviting her back.

When Rose got home she found a note from

Jack lying on the kitchen floor. He must have pushed it under the door. He had never learnt to telephone first, always wrongly assuming she'd be there if he needed or wanted to see her.

'. . . I'll be back around five if that's convenient. If not, leave a message on my voicemail,' he'd written.

Wrapped up warmly against the weather, Rose drove out to Porthcurnow and sketched the waves as they crashed against the jagged cliffs, sending spray high into the air. Below her, the golden sand was pristine; the earlier high tide had washed away any footprints. The beach was deserted, so different from the summer months when visitors abounded, especially when there was a production at the Minack theatre. It was an open-air construction, a tiered semicircle carved out of the cliff and with a spectacular view of the sea.

Deep in concentration, the next hour or so passed quickly. Only when her fingers, encased in fingerless gloves, became too cold to work did she decide it was time to go home.

There was Christmas to think about. Rarely did she bother with it unless her parents came to stay. In latter years that was infrequent, they usually took a cruise. This one would be different because it would be the first one her father would spend without her mother in all the years since they had been married. Rose knew she had to make it special for him, not by creating a fuss but by making sure he enjoyed it as far as was possible. How she could do that was a different matter.

Doreen Clarke had been beating butter and sugar for a cake when she heard the news on the radio. 'Poor little mite,' she said aloud. She was pleased her boys were men and out of that sort of danger even if they faced others. They both lived abroad, on different continents. As their father had been before them, they were miners, but since the last Cornish tin mine had closed down they had had to seek work elsewhere. Her husband, Cyril, had been made redundant a decade ago and, at fifty-one, had found himself too old for any other sort of work. His despondency did not last long. All his time was now invested in the garden surrounding their bungalow in Hayle. He could always find something to do whatever the season, whatever the weather. Many of their friends benefited from the produce he grew as well as from the flowers that flourished under his care.

Before she left for work the following morning

Doreen listened to the news again. The child still hadn't been found. She hoped Jack Pearce was on the case. He's a good man, and an 'ansome one, she thought, as if good looks could make any difference.

It was Wednesday, the only weekday when she had the afternoon to herself. As the house she was cleaning that morning was in Crowlas, on the road between Hayle and Newlyn, she decided she would call in and see Rose after she'd shopped in Penzance. They hadn't met up for a coffee in weeks. She would take some of Cyril's carrots, a Savoy and half a dozen of the firm skinned onions that Rose loved.

Rose was cleaning paintbrushes when Doreen arrived. She smiled at the sight of her friend. Short and dumpy and bundled up in her winter coat, Doreen resembled a cheerful gnome. Although junior to Rose by a month or so, she could pass for ten years older and had a habit of acting as if she was her mother. Her iron-grey hair was cut in an uncompromising chin length bob. Over her shoulder was slung the large bag that travelled everywhere with her. 'You've timed it well. I've just finished work for the day.'

'And I'm glad to find 'e in maid. I know you go out working in all weathers, just like my

Cyril. It's a wonder the pair of 'e don't catch your deaths. Here, take this bag, there's a bit of veg in it for you.'

Rose thanked her and filled the kettle. No way would Doreen leave before she'd had a cup of something. And Rose now had the time to listen to the latest gossip.

'You heard about Margaret Bishop, didn't you?'

Rose shook her head. She had no idea who Margaret Bishop was but that wouldn't stop Doreen recounting the tale of what had happened to her, or, more likely, what the woman had done.

'And now there's the awful news about that little girl, you must've heard about that,' Doreen continued when she had finished the story of adultery, made more scandalous in her view because it was being conducted with a younger man.

'Yes. I was there when it happened.'

'You were?' She leant forward, avid for news.

Rose gave her a brief account of the events of the previous afternoon.

'You'll have Jack on your back now, maid. You know what he's like, he's so protective of you.'

Protective? Rose did not see him in that light.

'I'm not in any danger, Doreen. My name wasn't given to the press and whoever he is; the man won't be interested in me. All I hope is that they find her alive.'

'We all hope that.'

Rose did not add that she had been to see Beth's mother. She didn't want that bit of information being passed on. She liked Doreen enormously but there were limits to how much she was prepared to confide in her. As Doreen continued to chat Rose wondered if she ought to mention it to Jack. It was probably best to be honest but she knew what anger such an admission might well arouse.

CHAPTER THREE

Doreen and Jack must have passed on the road for he tapped on the kitchen window only minutes after she'd left. He knew he looked tired. It had been a very late night. But any decent person, let alone a policeman, would sacrifice sleep to search for a missing child.

Rose opened the door. 'Come in, Jack. Would you like a drink or some tea?'

'It had better be tea. I could be called back in at any time.'

Rose kissed his cheek, standing on her toes to do so. He was almost a foot taller than her. A faint smell of aftershave remained in the stubble, which had appeared since he had shaved that morning. 'I take it this isn't purely social,' she said as she filled the kettle. It was evening now as far as she was concerned and she'd had her fill of tea with Doreen. It was certainly dark outside, therefore time for a glass of the dry white wine she enjoyed after a day's work.

'Not entirely. Someone else could have come but it was an excuse to see you. I suppose I was also half hoping you might've remembered a few more details regarding yesterday afternoon.'

She pulled off the band that held her hair back in a ponytail. It had been wound too tightly and her head was beginning to ache. 'I've been thinking of nothing else all day. That's it, Jack. What I told the officer yesterday is all I know. Is there any chance of finding her?'

'What can I say? Your guess is as good as mine here.'

'I went to see Sally Jones this morning.' Instantly, she saw the tightening of his mouth. 'And before you say anything, she, or, rather, her sister rang to ask me to go over there. I don't really know why. Anyway, I would have thought your PC in residence there would have told you that already.'

No one had told him. All telephone calls and visitors to Sally's address were supposed to be monitored. Someone would be in trouble, either

Janice Richards for not reporting it or the officer who had taken the message but failed to pass it on. 'So what was the outcome?' Jack was fully aware that he could not control her actions, Rose had always made that perfectly clear.

'There wasn't an outcome exactly. I think she needed someone to talk to other than a policewoman. All Sally could think of by way of explanation was that I was the last person to see Beth. She looks dreadful, Jack, but no wonder. I can understand what she must be going through.'

'Can you?'

Rose bit her lip. Was he being deliberately cruel in referring to her lack of children, or was it simply an unthinking comment because he'd had a hard twenty-four hours? She decided to give him the benefit of the doubt. Now was not the time for an argument.

'No doubt you'll be going to see her again.' He held up his hands, the palms facing Rose as if to ward off a verbal attack. 'Not that I can stop you if that's what she wants. But isn't it enough that you turn out to be the only witness? I really despair of you sometimes, Rose.'

'Look, Jack, it was through no fault of my own that I happened to be on the beach at Marazion. Even you have to accept that.'

'Yes. I do.' He took the mug of tea she handed him. 'I wish this had never happened, I wish I was here because we were going out for the evening. There are times when I hate this bloody job.'

She was aware of the reason for his mood. He was dreading the worst scenario and was powerless to do something about it if it had already taken place.

'Look, are you absolutely certain that Beth went with this man willingly?'

Rose nodded. 'I'm positive.' There was no way in which she had been mistaken. The child had held up its arms and asked to be carried. Unless there was another explanation. 'Jack, is it possible that a four-year-old girl, one who's used to being with people, one who isn't in the least bit shy, would have no fear in going off with a stranger? Could he be one of those men who offer sweets or some other treat and she simply trusted him enough to go with him?'

'It seems unlikely, but you never know. These days mothers warn their children about such dangers while they're still in their prams.' But it does still happen, he reminded himself.

Rose thought about other explanations. Carol claimed Sally was virtually alcoholic. Suppose she was the sort of mother never to have issued such warnings, a mother who took strange men into her home so her daughter had become used to them? Or had she been drunk or partially so yesterday and not watching Beth as well as she ought to have done? Except her breath didn't smell of alcohol, Rose recalled, and she had been close enough to have noticed. None of this did she mention to Jack. For a start there was only Carol's word for it and the bottle Rose had seen may have been less than half full to begin with. It was not a logical thought but Rose felt vaguely responsible for what had happened to little Bethany Jones, as if, in some way she could have prevented it.

Jack's pager bleeped. 'May I use the phone?' He asked because he never took advantage of her hospitality.

'Of course you can.'

'They've let the father go,' he told her when he had finished the call. 'His name's Michael Poole.' Jack knew that anything he told her would go no further, that despite her ability to get into trouble, her overdeveloped sense of curiosity and one or two other irritating habits, Rose was totally trustworthy as well as being a true and loyal friend to those she liked. As she had visited Sally Jones she was probably already aware of the father's name.

'Was he arrested?'

'No. We kept an eye on him overnight then someone interviewed him at his firm's head office in Plymouth. He was devastated and volunteered to go to Charles Cross police station to make a statement. He's been advised against coming down here just in case whoever has Beth decides to get in touch with him. Everyone's been advised to carry on as much as normal, which is pretty ridiculous under the circumstances, but we need the people involved to be contactable just in case.'

'You think Beth's been kidnapped?'

'She's certainly been abducted but I doubt there's any ransom involved. The mother's almost penniless, apart from any benefits she might be claiming, and Poole's in a good job but not one that will make him rich.' He sighed. 'I just don't know, Rose. If a relative hasn't snatched a child and there's no ransom demand these cases turn out to be about sexual abuse or murder. Sometimes both.'

Rose recalled what Sally had said about Michael Poole continuing to support his child. 'But is she on benefits? Sally told me that Beth's father still pays for her keep regularly.'

'What do you mean?'

Rose blushed, ashamed of her thoughts. 'Perhaps she's claiming as well.'

Jack frowned. 'You're not making any sense, Rose.'

'When I was at Sally's, one of the things she said was that she didn't want anything more to do with Beth's father, which was the reason she'd moved away from Looe. It surprised me that he carries on paying when he doesn't have any access to Beth.'

This sounded a little too altruistic to be true. 'Was Janice Richards aware of this comment?' If this were the case there could be two reasons for her being in trouble.

'No, I don't think she was, actually. I'm sure she'd gone to use the bathroom at the time. Why? Is it important?' Even before she'd finished asking she realised that it might be. If Michael Poole was still making payments to Sally it was possible that she was guilty of benefit fraud. But surely there would be checks made on a newcomer to an area before the DHSS started handing out money.

'It certainly could be. It's something to look into.' Not much of a start, though, except Jack was beginning to think that the case was not as simple as it appeared. 'I think I'll go now. I'm going to try and get a couple of hours sleep. I'm shattered.'

That he left without kissing her or arranging

another time to see her showed Rose just how concerned he was.

After he'd left she felt restless and would normally have sought Laura's company, but Trevor had landed and would want to spend time with his wife. Rose smiled. Well, not necessarily. Although he was at sea for days on end, their reunions were not always harmonious. Trevor would be tired as he, like many other fishermen, worked in shifts, four hours on, four hours off, and once Laura, who worried about him continuously whilst he was at sea, knew he was safe, she was not one of the most patient of women. She had always been the same. It was her nature; just as her nervous energy and vibrancy was a part of the whole that made Laura what she was. Rose envied her ability to eat whatever she wanted and to remain thin.

I'll ring Barry Rowe and see if he fancies a drink, she decided. He answered the phone on the second ring. Maybe he had hoped it was Jenny calling. To save him embarrassment, Rose asked if he'd arranged to meet her that night.

'No, not this evening,' he said. 'She's babysitting. Are you about to invite me somewhere sophisticated and exciting?'

'Such as where?'

'Ah, I get your point. Just a drink I take it?'

'That's what I had in mind. How about the Alex in half an hour?'

'Ideal. I'll see you soon.'

The Alexandra Inn and Alexandra Road in which it was situated, were named after one of Queen Victoria's daughters who had once visited the area. It was about halfway between Newlyn and the shop in Penzance above which Barry lived which meant they could both walk the distance easily.

It was a clear night with the tang of kelp in the air. The beach was littered with thick wads of seaweed. Sometimes there was none at all; it depended upon the ebb and flow of the tide and the roughness of the sea. Overhead, stars glittered sharply and a full moon shone on the blackness of the water in the bay, lighting up a container ship, which lay beneath its circle. Beyond it was what looked like a frigate, but Rose couldn't be certain. The wind had dropped but there was a rolling swell which made the silvery reflection of the moon undulate. In the distance a curlew cried as it took flight from its resting place.

No matter what time of the year, no matter what time of the day or night, Rose never tired of the beauty before her. She would not, could not, ever leave the area now.

When she arrived Barry was already at the bar. There were several other customers; those who called in after work. But it was too early for the people who went home to eat first. Rose knew most of them. This was typical of the area, everyone knew everyone else and their business and it was a foolish person who gossiped in public because the man or woman standing right behind you was likely to be a relative of the person under discussion.

It was warm in the pub. The thick, lined curtains were drawn against the winter evening. The click of balls meant that a game of pool was underway in the other bar.

'Dry white?' Barry asked as he pushed his thick-rimmed glasses back into place. As long as Rose had known him he had never owned glasses that fitted him properly.

Barry ordered her drink. He already had a pint of one of the several real ales on offer in front of him. The pub had built up a reputation for good beer and excellent food, which the landlady made herself from fresh, local ingredients. 'So, to what do I owe this honour?' As Barry smiled several lines creased his wide forehead, above which was his slightly thinning hair. Rose noticed it was no longer in need of a cut.

'I don't know really. I just felt like getting out.'

Rose had never been afraid of going anywhere alone. Like many women locally, whose husbands were at sea, she felt no shyness or embarrassment in visiting any of the pubs without an escort. And it was perfectly safe to do so. This made Barry wonder why she had specifically wanted his company.

Rose hoisted herself on to one of the high but comfortable bar stools and then, because it was so much on her mind, she told Barry about Beth.

He listened carefully then sighed. 'Don't get involved, Rose. You know there's nothing you can do.'

'But I'm already involved. I can't stop thinking about her. She's out there somewhere, maybe cold or terrified or hurt.'

Barry knew he was defeated; that nothing he could say would stop her becoming more involved. He sipped his beer whilst he thought about it. 'Let me put it this way then, what do you actually intend doing?'

'I might go and see Norma Penhalligon. There's something not quite right. I can't put my finger on it but I think she might know something.' She sighed. 'Enough of this; how's Jenny?'

Rose had learnt a lot about Jenny Rogers

during the short time she had known her. After an unhappy marriage she had divorced. Nichola, now twenty-one, was her only child. Nichola had become a single parent eighteen months ago and adored her own daughter, Polly, but she refused to name the father. Jenny guessed that this was because he was married rather than because she didn't know his identity. Her daughter was not promiscuous. Either way, both women loved Polly.

It had been a surprise to Rose to watch the easy way in which Barry responded to the child. Perhaps his total lack of experience in that respect precluded any preformed ideas regarding children and had prevented inhibitions in their company to have taken hold.

Two single mothers, Rose thought, two women she had recently come into contact with, yet they had so very little in common.

They talked shop for a while; Rose's ideas for the greetings cards, Barry's plans to increase his range of stock the following summer, then they both decided they were hungry.

'It's fish and chips for me tonight,' Barry said as they left the bar. 'Would you like me to walk you home first?'

'No, thanks. I'll be fine.' She wanted to be alone

now to think. Something Doreen Clarke had said was bothering her. Just what it was she couldn't remember. She had not been concentrating fully at the time because occasionally, when Doreen was in full flow, it was necessary to switch off for a while. The words were more likely to come back to her if she tried to think of other things.

The wind had risen slightly and was now blowing gently off the sea. A few clouds were blown across the bay temporarily obscuring the moon. Towards Newlyn a trawler chugged into view and made the turn ready to sail into the harbour. The fishermen would remain on board until they had landed their fish in the morning.

When she reached home she made her daily call to her father then completed the crossword in the *Western Morning News* whilst she waited for her meal to cook. It felt strange, not being at the gallery annexe taking her class on a Wednesday evening.

The following morning, as Rose walked down through Newlyn and along the Promenade towards Morrab Gardens, the sky was a clear blue with a small bank of white cloud in the distance. Barry required some new watercolours for the notelets he produced. They were always simple designs, usually a single wild flower on a plain background. Now and then Rose would portray a huddle of cottages around a church, a disused mine stack or one of the tiny fishing villages with their steeply sloping streets and quaint harbours. However, having discussed it with Barry the previous night she had decided upon another local feature; the subtropical plants which flourished in the area. There were many varieties in Morrab Gardens; palms which grew to ten or twelve feet high and had massive flowers in the spring and summer, and succulents with their fleshy leaves ranging in shades from palest green to black.

In her battered canvas satchel were sketchpads and pencils, her fingerless gloves and a small waterproof sheet in case the benches were damp.

Choosing a seat near the fountain Rose studied a palm tree, one of the Phoenix families, although she wasn't sure which. Its shape, outlined against the sky, was ideal for what she had in mind.

Well protected by layers of clothes and surrounded by tall trees and many shrubs she was sheltered from the wind and was therefore able to work for over an hour before the cold began to penetrate. She watched a herring gull stamping the grass to bring the worms to the surface. A grey wagtail darted around the stonework of the fountain, its white edged, and blackish tail bobbing up and down continuously. It reminded her of Doreen who was always bustling. And Doreen reminded her of Norma Penhalligon.

It was just after ten thirty. By the time she walked home, got the car and drove to Marazion Norma would probably have done her shopping and it would surely be too early to be disturbing her at lunch. Now was the ideal time to go. She packed up her sketches and started to walk home, wondering just when it was she had decided for certain that she would pay the woman a visit.

She was dressed in jeans, boots, a thick checked shirt and a heavy sweater. Over this she wore a padded jacket. But she didn't imagine Norma would be offended by her informality. At least her hair was tidy, held back at the nape of her neck by a tortoiseshell clip.

When Norma let Rose into the house she showed no surprise at seeing her. She merely smiled as if she had known she would return then ushered her in through the door leading to her flat. It was almost as Rose had imagined it to be. The furniture was made from a dark wood and looked old and well used. There was an arrangement of dried flowers on the sideboard and some framed photographs and china ornaments scattered over various surfaces. Heavy curtains hung at the windows. A fire blazed in the grate, throwing out more heat than seemed possible. This room probably reflected they way the whole house had once looked in the Victorian era when it was built.

'I had a feeling you might be back. Shall we have some tea?'

'That'd be nice. Thank you.'

'You sit down, I'll go and fetch it.'

Norma had been more welcoming than Rose had expected. She sat in one of the deep leather armchairs with its brass studs. It was scuffed in places but still very comfortable. The whole room had a comfortable atmosphere as if many people had relaxed in it. Apart from the cheerful fire there were small tables beside both armchairs and at either end of the matching settee. Each of them held an ashtray, a reading lamp and a coaster. There would be no need to reach far for anything in Norma's flat.

I'm here now, but what do I say? Rose asked herself. Hopefully Mrs Penhalligon would lead the conversation.

Surprisingly, the tea did not come in cups on a tray but in two mugs. One proclaimed 'I love my grandma'; the one that was handed to Rose advertised a brand of instant coffee. 'Do you take sugar, maid?' Norma enquired.

'No, thanks.'

'Just as well. Neither do I. I usually keep some in for guests but I've run out.' She sat down heavily and rubbed a knee beneath her cord trousers. 'Now, I suppose this is about little Beth. You're not happy with the situation, are you?'

Rose was amazed that she could have seen that on such a short acquaintanceship.

Norma nodded and patted her greying hair, checking for wayward curls. 'I saw it in your face. You were worried, of course, but you were puzzled, too.'

'Well, who wouldn't be worried? It was, well, actually it was something the sister said.'

'Ah, Carol. I can't make that one out. Sally's as straightforward as they're ever likely to come and she can't do enough for Beth, but for some reason I don't trust that Carol.' She paused. 'What exactly did she say to you?'

Rose swallowed some tea. It was very strong and made with full cream milk and tasted awful. 'Obviously you won't repeat this, but Carol suggested her sister was an alcoholic.'

Norma snorted. 'Never. What ever put that idea into her head? The girl likes the occasional drink, but who doesn't? As far as I'm aware she has a couple in the evening once Beth's in bed. She can't get out unless

I babysit and that's not often because she hasn't had a chance to make any real friends yet. I know it's only my opinion but I'm sure Carol's wrong.'

How could she be so sure? Carol would know Sally better than Norma did, and Norma couldn't possibly be aware of what was going on upstairs twenty-four hours a day. Yet Rose believed her. Norma had quickly discerned that Rose was troubled, and she came across as a woman of good sense, one with an ability to sum people up accurately on a single meeting.

'What do you think is going on?'

'I don't know, Mrs Penhalligon, but something just doesn't feel right.'

'That's my impression, too. Sally told me that the child's father tried to obtain custody even though he'd never have been able to look after her himself, not without giving up his job. He'd got it into his head that Sally wasn't looking after her properly. She told me it was awful, Social Services nosing around all the time. Obviously he didn't get anywhere with it.'

'It's almost as if there's some sort of conspiracy against her.' Rose voiced her thoughts aloud before realising they were overexaggerated. 'Not conspiracy exactly, but it's as if she isn't meant to keep Beth.'

'It does, seem that way, although I heard on the news that Beth's father is in the clear.'

'I know, Jack told me.'

'Jack? You mean Inspector Pearce?'

'Yes. He's a friend of mine.'

'You could have worse friends than that.' Norma smiled. 'More than a friend from what I gather. There's no need to blush, maid. I know Amelia Pearce. We were at school together.'

It should not have surprised Rose, who had lived in West Penwith long enough to realise these things always happened. She had met Jack's mother on several occasions, although she didn't encourage visitors and rarely left the village of Paul where she lived. Rose liked her and admired her independence. 'She's by no means a recluse; she's simply one of those people who prefer their own company to anyone else's,' Jack had once told her.

Amelia Pearce had been warm and friendly and took an interest in Rose's work. On that first visit Amelia had cooked them pasties, the best that Rose had ever tasted. The pastry was light and they were made in the traditional manner; the meat, beef skirt, at one end, potato and swede at the other. Some insisted that the meat should be on top in order that the juices ran into the vegetables but Amelia had managed to make them do so anyway.

'He's a good lad, is Jack. I'm glad he's in charge of the case.' Norma's smile faded. 'It's been two days now.'

Rose knew what she was thinking but didn't want to put it in words herself. 'I wish there was something we could do to help.'

'I suppose we could go and see Carol. To offer our moral support? I called on Sally this morning but she doesn't want any visitors. Besides, her mother's with her now. She closed up the shop and came straight down even though Sally said not to.'

Offer moral support? What a strange suggestion. Norma must have an ulterior motive. Rose had met Carol only briefly, it was hardly enough of an excuse to turn up uninvited. Norma knew her a little better which made Rose wonder if she had suspicions regarding the sister. Jack, or someone, would have interviewed her, that much was certain, but it was often the case that people were less guarded in their speech when dealing with those who were not in authority. Or am I fooling myself? she wondered. Am I just hoping that I can put things right? 'When did you have in mind?' She had committed herself now.

'No time like the present. We could stop and have a late lunch on the way back. You'll have to drive, dear. I don't have a car any longer. She lives some way out of Marazion, it's too far to walk.'

'That's fine.' Giving Norma a lift would give her the perfect excuse for being there. Rose stood and put on her coat then waited for Norma to clear away the mugs and fetch her own coat from where ever she kept it. Then, together, they went out to the car.

There was some congestion in the narrow streets as two double-decker buses tried to pass as they made their individual ways to and from Helston, but soon they were winding through country lanes, going up hill, away from the sea. 'I think it's the next left,' Norma said. 'I've only been there the once.'

'Oh?' Rose wondered why she should have been there at all.

'Carol came over to pick Sally up one day and asked if I fancied a ride, too.' She grinned. 'I went, just out of curiosity.'

Rose glanced at Norma's profile and grinned back. 'Yes. I can understand that.' They certainly had one thing in common.

They pulled up on the verge outside the bungalow. It would be rude to open the gate and drive in. Besides, the wheels would mess up the immaculately raked gravel in the drive. Here we go, Rose thought, praying that she wasn't about to end up in a situation she would rather have avoided.

CHAPTER FOUR

Doreen Clarke was wiping down the surfaces in her tidy kitchen. She and Cyril regularly ate their main meal of the day at twelve thirty. Since his redundancy he had become a reasonable plain cook and had their food ready to be served when Doreen returned from one or other of her morning cleaning jobs. Once they had eaten she would rinse and stack the dishes then leave them for Cyril to wash after she'd left for work again.

Still clutching the dishcloth, her plump and reddened hand rested on the kitchen table. Driving home earlier she had passed Susan Overton who was on the way to school to collect her daughter, Katy, and take her home for lunch.

Susan's face showed she was still troubled. She had not responded when Doreen tooted her horn.

I mentioned it to Rose, Doreen thought, strange she never commented. 'T'aint like that maid not to speak her mind. She's usually got an opinion on most things. Doreen realised she would be late if she didn't leave at once. She turned to Cyril. 'I'll be off then, love. See you later.'

Cyril, seated at the table, was reading a paper, his lunchtime glass of brown ale to hand. The kitchen smelt of grilled lamb chops. Their lives had developed a ritualistic pattern. Maybe it was a reaction to the disruption Cyril's shift work in the mine had caused. He glanced up at his wife and smiled. 'I'll be here.' He didn't resent preparing her meals. Doreen was now the breadwinner. Although he was more than ten years older than her, he wouldn't receive his state pension for another four years and the interest from his redundancy payoff didn't go far. Doreen had always looked after him and the boys in the past and had taken part-time work when they were older. Now it was his turn; what he did went a little way towards repaying her. With the garden and his weekly game of darts and bowls in the summer he was never bored. Bossy, and a bit of a gossip, she might be, but Cyril loved and admired his hardworking wife. Doreen left the bungalow and got into her car, straightening the pleats of her woollen skirt beneath her as she slid into the driver's seat. She never had nor ever would wear jeans or trousers. Her overall was neatly folded in her bag. I'll speak to Rose again, she decided. I'm sure she'll know what I ought to do.

Laura Penfold was annoyed. Trevor had hardly set foot on land before he was off again. First he'd gone fishing. Like many other fishermen he also used a rod and line by way of a hobby and was quite prepared to sit on the beach in all weathers, even throughout a winter's night in the rain. Having returned without catching anything he had slept for a while before announcing that they needed some spares for the boat and that he was going out to buy them. 'Which means you'll call in at the Swordfish on your way home,' she had added sarcastically to his retreating back, regretting it immediately because if that had not been his intention, he would certainly do so now.

Trevor did not respond. This was no indication of his own mood; he saved his words for when he had something important to say. Laura was the garrulous one.

It was just after four. Trevor might be gone for several hours. 'Bugger him,' she said. 'I'll see if Rose fancies a drink.'

Ten past four in the afternoon might seem early to be thinking of such a thing but in Newlyn, as in other fishing ports, lives were lived on a different timescale. The pubs were open all day because fishermen who had been at sea for days on end were more than ready for a drink when they landed, even if it was ten thirty in the morning. And the fish buyers would have been up since long before dawn. To such people four o'clock would be the equivalent of eight p.m. to office workers who kept to more regular hours. And there were the early risers like Laura; and Rose, who might already have worked a full day by that time.

Laura tapped out the number and waited. She was disappointed when the answering machine clicked on. Then, over the recorded message, she heard a muffled 'Damn. Hold on a minute.' The message stopped playing. 'Hello?'

'Hi, there. It's me.'

'Sorry about that. I've just got in. I couldn't quite make it to the phone.'

'Been anywhere exciting?'

'Exciting, no, but interesting and rather worrying.'

'Want to tell Aunty Laura all about it over a drink?'

'That sounds like a good idea.' As far as she was aware Laura didn't know of her involvement in Beth's disappearance. Not a particular fan of radio and television she may not even know that a child was missing. 'Is Trevor coming?'

'Bollocks to Trevor. This is girls only.'

Another row, Rose thought, unsurprised. They would make up as quickly as they had fallen out if past form was any guide. It was the pattern of their lives. 'Where shall we meet?'

'The Star. I'm on my way, I'll see you when you get there.' Laura hung up. She pulled an old duffel coat on over her leggings and chunky sweater, locked the house then walked down the hill through the lanes too narrow for traffic. Hers was a small back-to-back property in one of the lanes off Chywoone Hill. It was the house in which she and Trevor had managed to bring up their three boys, all of whom had left home and moved away to find work. Like most of the old fishermen's cottages it was built from granite and had no garden, only a yard. The net loft had been converted into a bedroom and the kitchen and bathroom had long since been modernised.

She reached the bottom of the hill and turned

left to the Strand where the Star stood opposite the fish market, which was now shuttered. Almost adjacent was the Swordfish, where Trevor would be heading later. There was no guessing how busy the pubs would be at any given time. If most of the boats had landed or the weather was too rough for fishing they could be crowded by mid-morning and empty again by late afternoon. Conversely, if the weather and tides were right there would be few customers. When Laura walked in there were about twenty people standing around the bar, most of whom she knew. She asked for a house gin and tonic, which meant a double, just as Rose arrived. 'I think I'll have the same for a change,' she said.

They moved away from the bar and stood near a pillar that supported a small shelf upon which they could place their glasses. It was a basic pub with wooden floors and a few tables and plastic covered benches; a place where working men could drink in their overalls and dirty boots without fear of mud or fish scales ruining a carpet or the furniture.

'What's up with you and Trevor, then?

Laura tossed back her long, dark, corkscrew curls and sniffed. 'The usual. I've hardly seen him since he's been back and he's sailing again tomorrow night.'

Rose did not suggest that it might be a good idea for Laura to be at home for when he did return. It would have been a waste of breath, just as any advice Laura gave Rose concerning Jack would have been.

'So, tell me about your interesting day.'

'Did you hear about that little girl that's gone missing?'

'Yes. Have they found her yet?'

Rose shook her head sadly before describing her part in it.

'My God, that's typical of you. I should've known.'

'There's more. After I went to see Sally I decided to go and see Norma Penhalligon. She talked me into going to Carol's place.'

'The sister? Whatever for? Rose, do I really want to hear this? I mean, what on earth's Jack going to think?'

'He knows I saw Sally,' she answered defensively.

'Well, go on, tell me the rest.'

Carol's modern bungalow was some way out of Marazion. It had a small garden and was surrounded by countryside but with no view of the sea. 'Obviously she wasn't expecting us, but she asked us in. The whole time we were there she

70

seemed a bit flustered. She doesn't work because she can't find anything to fit in with her children's school hours and there aren't any neighbours to look after them until she gets home.'

'What's that got to do with anything?'

Rose shrugged. 'Beats me, but she seemed keen that we should know. She said if she did find something she'd have to pay a childminder, which would defeat the whole object.'

'But why did you go there in the first place?'

'I just felt there was something not quite right, and Norma had the same impression. We thought she might let something slip. People do, without meaning to.'

'Especially when you're around.'

Rose smiled, she knew this was true but had never understood the reason for it. 'Anyway, the place was spotless and there weren't any signs of children around; no toys or anything.'

'Some people aren't sluts like me, you know.'

'You're hardly that. Untidy, I'll grant you. No, this was almost obsessively clean, no ornaments, no photographs, nothing.'

'So what?'

'It felt wrong. When we got there Norma asked if there was anything she could do, babysit, maybe, if she wanted to go and see Sally, but

Carol refused and said she was quite capable of coping and that her husband was due back as soon as a flight was available.'

'Look, Rose, if there is something strange about Carol, you definitely ought to keep out of it. You know you'll end up in trouble. Get Jack to take you out, he'll soon put you right.' Fat chance of that, Laura thought, but he might be able to warn her off.

It was quiet without the children. Tamsin and Lucy were staying with John's parents in Penzance. They had been more than willing to have them for a night or two, not only because it was fun and they loved them, they also made them feel young. They could not have guessed what would happen to Beth but it now gave their daughter-in-law a chance to be with her sister who would need her more than ever.

That, at least, was what Carol had told them. She stood in the recess of the lounge window and watched as the increasing darkness altered the shape of the landscape. Fields and hedges merged into one and the bare branches of the trees, to which a few leaves still clung, were silhouetted against the skyline. It was not Beth of whom she was thinking, nor was it John. She did not know how she felt about him. It was Marcus, the man with whom she was having an affair, who held her attention.

She turned and walked across the room, flicking on the light switch as she passed it. Twice she entered all the rooms of the ranch style bungalow and checked the surfaces for dust even though she cleaned the place thoroughly every morning. It was a home in which no one was allowed to wear the same clothes for more than a day. John's working clothes went through two cycles in the washing machine, the sheets were changed twice a week, yet, to Carol, nothing ever seemed really clean.

In the kitchen she noticed a small splash of something on the tiles between the worktop and the overhead cupboards. She wetted a cloth with disinfectant and wiped it away. The cloth was rinsed thoroughly before being folded and placed over the rim of the washing up bowl beneath the sink.

She would be seeing Marcus tonight, but only briefly. It seemed a waste when John was away, but it had to be that way. However, Carol knew the affair was about to end. It could not continue any longer. What she would do afterwards she had yet to decide.

Her eye caught the kitchen telephone extension.

She must ring Sally. She didn't really want to but knew that she had to. How callous it would seem not to make the call. It was her mother who answered.

With a tearful voice she said, 'Oh, Carol, I feel so helpless. Sally's almost out of her mind. I called the doctor but she refuses to take the tablets he's given her. I just wish they would find her. Who could possibly do such a thing to an innocent child?'

'Don't take on, Mum, it won't help. Does Sally want me to come over?' There was time for a quick visit.

There was a mumbled conversation. 'No, love, leave it until tomorrow. She's had enough for one day.'

'Well, ring me if you need me.'

'We will.'

Carol paced the bungalow once more. She had some decisions to make and she had to make them quickly.

Outside, somewhere beneath the moon which was just beginning to wane, an owl hooted. Moonlight and owls went together. That night they seemed more eerie than romantic. They echoed her melancholy mood.

* * *

Jack and his team had no idea where to turn next. The searches were still continuing and requests had gone out via the media asking people, especially farmers, to search their sheds and outhouses. On the afternoon of Beth's disappearance roadblocks had been set up at the Tamar Bridge and the only alternative route out of the county, the small bridge at Gunnislake. The mainline station in Penzance had been alerted; the staff asked to watch out for a man with a child of Beth's description. Her abductor would not have had time to make it as far as the roadblocks even though over an hour had elapsed by the time the police had responded to the call and questioned the people on the beach. Time enough, though, for the man to have driven to Penzance or Camborne station and caught the 15.12 train from the former or the same train when it arrived at the latter at 16.14. This was a Paddington train. Jack had had the foresight to make sure all fourteen stations after Penzance were aware of the situation. No sightings had been reported. He had known that this was unlikely, that if you had a car you did not catch a train, but he could not afford to take any risks. There was no other feasible way out of Cornwall; flights from Land's End and Newquay airports had to be booked in advance and getting away by boat suggested drastic planning. The scene Rose had described seemed more of a spur of the moment thing.

Jack sat in his ground floor flat in Morrab Road. It was spacious, with high ceilings, one of a pair into which the solidly built property had been converted and was situated between other flats and the offices of solicitors, dentists and alternative health practitioners.

It was past midnight but he was no longer tired; his mind was too active for sleep. All the people on the beach had been interviewed again, as had all of Beth's relatives, and, of course, Rose. He wished she were there with him. He could have lain down beside her even if sleep still eluded him.

What next? he thought. What the bloody hell can we do next?

Katy was undressed ready for bed. She had hardly touched her tea again. Her six-year-old face, which should have been smiling, was white and pinched. Susan had tried everything she could think of to get her daughter to talk.

'There's nothing wrong, Mummy,' was all she would say.

But Susan knew her daughter well. No longer

was she that happy, outgoing child she had been. Something was terribly wrong. She had her suspicions, but how could she voice them? Who on earth could she turn to if what she thought turned out to be correct? And if she did voice them and she turned out to be wrong it would cause nothing but trouble for everyone. But she had to know. The doctor had found nothing physically wrong with Katy, which was some sort of relief; it was her mental state which bothered Susan. 'Would you like to watch some television?'

'No, Mummy. I'm tired. I want to go to bed.'

It was only six o'clock but Katy did look washed out. That was how Doreen Clarke had put it. 'You want to take her to the doctor, maid. And if you ask me, there'd be no harm in him taking a look at you as well,' she had said. Susan had taken Doreen's advice but it hadn't solved the problem. 'Come on then. I'll read you a story.'

Together they went up the stairs. Susan had almost finished reading when she heard the front door open. Simon was home. He commuted to Truro where he ran a financial advisory service. She heard him drop his briefcase by the table on the woodblock floor of the hall. He would hang up his coat in the downstairs cloakroom then seek her out. She had always been grateful for his tidiness. She kissed Katy, pulled the duvet around her shoulders, and then went downstairs to greet her husband.

'Hello, there,' he said as she entered the kitchen. There was no welcoming aroma of cooking, no sign, in fact, that there was going to be any food. He took a deep breath. Neither his wife nor his child had much to say to him these days. 'We need to talk, love.' He pulled out a stool from beneath the breakfast counter. 'Sit down, I'll pour us a drink.'

Susan hoped that the alcohol would help quell, rather than increase, the nausea she constantly felt. It had to come out; she had to tell Simon about her suspicions. What it would do to him she couldn't begin to guess.

'Is Katy in bed?' She nodded as Simon handed her her drink. 'So early?' He joined her at the breakfast counter.

Susan's stomach churned. 'She said she was tired.'

'Susan, what have I done? Why are you shutting me out like this?' He assumed Katy's attitude towards him was a reflection of her mother's.

'Nothing, you haven't done anything, Simon. It's just that I'm worried sick about Katy. You must've seen how she's changed.'

'You've both changed. I really thought it was something I'd done. I know I've been late home a few times lately but I'm trying to keep ahead of the game by ringing people at home when they get in from work.' He reached for her hand and squeezed it. 'You do know that there's never been anyone else but you, don't you?' He stood. 'I'll just kiss Katy goodnight and then you can tell me all about it.'

Dazed, Susan knew she would have to do so, that she would have to tell Simon that Katy had only changed since his younger brother had been to stay.

CHAPTER FIVE

'Morale is lousy here,' Jack told Rose when he rang from his office the following morning. 'Whatever happens today I'm having a few hours off. I can't keep going at this rate for much longer. I don't think any of us can. Anyway, the reason I'm calling is to see if you're free for dinner tonight. Arthur as well, if he's up to it.'

'That sounds great, Jack. I'll speak to Dad right away. Shall I book somewhere?'

'Yes, wherever you like. Make it for around seven if you can, I need a fairly early night.'

Rose could picture his handsome face, probably now grey with fatigue, and realised how much she felt for him. Until they argued, of course. But she still wasn't ready to commit herself and wondered whether she ever would be. She said goodbye, hung up and dialled her father's number. He took a long time to answer. It worried her. He could be out or in the bath but since her mother's death she frequently feared the worst.

'I'd really love to join you, as long as you don't mind me playing gooseberry,' Arthur said when he finally answered the phone. He had responded in the affirmative so quickly that Rose wondered just how lonely he was. He tried not to show it, nor to make any demands upon her time, but she knew exactly what he must be going through, and he had lived with her mother twice as long as she had done with David. At least he was no longer hundreds of miles away. And thankfully, through his previous visits, he already knew quite a lot of people in the area. 'We'll call for you about half six. There's no need to dress up.' Rose had decided upon Chinese. They all enjoyed it and Jack would be too exhausted to appreciate a more formalised meal. Several new restaurants had opened in Penzance over the past year or so, including one owned by the hotelier and sixties ex-supermodel, Jean Shrimpton, and her husband.

Although it was still very early she tried ringing the restaurant and left a message and her number on their answering service. As she hung up, Rose realised that it was Friday and that time was running out for Bethany Jones. She tried not to think about it.

There was work to be done; some general housework, which she loathed, washing to go into the machine and then the choice of sketching some more wild flowers, planning the next oil painting or taking some photographs. Few people realised that the quality of the light in Cornwall could be as clear in the winter as in the summer. But how else could the postcards of St Ives or Hayle Towans, for instance, show a blue sky, a turquoise sea fringed with white spume, cliffs adorned by palm trees above the fine, pale gold of the sand whilst the beaches were devoid of people? That day was such a day. Rose decided not to waste it. She would work outside somewhere. When the light altered she would continue in the attic.

It was so mild it might have been May. Throughout the month there had been rain and a few days of gale force winds but the real storms would come later, probably in January.

Rose programmed the washing machine,

hoovered and dusted each room and cleaned the bathroom. Once the clothes and linen were flapping on the line strung between the shed and the branch of a tree, she collected her gear from the larder leading off the kitchen. With a fridge and a freezer installed, the old marble shelves had long since become redundant. The room now served as storage space.

She had mistimed her departure. The roads were busy; not that there were any traffic jams – they only occurred in the height of the summer. She drove to Hayle and parked on the wasteland by the old harbour. She took out her satchel, locked the car and walked to the top of the Towans. From where she stood, her feet slipping in the powdery sand which was held in place by the gently waving marram grass, she saw only the sparkle of the sea, now aquamarine, the greenness of the land on the opposite bank of the mouth of the River Hayle and the whiteness of the beach. The colours of nature defied description. Not a solitary person was in sight, not a single bird could be seen. The only sounds were the gentle lapping of the incoming tide against the shore and the whisper of the grasses as an unfelt breeze stirred them.

Rose adjusted her camera and looked through

the viewfinder. 'Oh, perfect,' she said after her second shot when a small fishing vessel entered the mouth of the river, its sole crewman at the tiller. She took several more shots in quick succession, not wishing the boat to be in the centre of the photograph. It would draw the eye and thus detract from the beauty of the scenery and it would also appear too contrived. Already the morning had produced satisfying results.

There was plenty of time to drive to the other side of St Ives Bay and, hopefully, achieve similar results.

At Carbis Bay the breeze was more noticeable and there were small waves breaking. The surf was nowhere near strong enough for actual surfing, which usually took place on one of the other beaches even during the winter now that wetsuits were freely available.

The few walkers on the beach, wearing jackets or jumpers, gave a surreal quality to the scene when contrasted against the blue sky and golden sand. A dog ran in and out of the white froth running up the sand, barking ecstatically as it did so. A small child ran to join it. Rose stood very still and only realised she had been holding her breath when a woman ran after her, scolding her for getting her shoes wet. For a split second she had imagined the child was alone. It was then she recalled what Doreen had mentioned.

Doreen knew Susan Overton who was the daughter of Ann Pascoe, the lady who gave Rose's hair its twice yearly trim. Rose and Ann were not friends in the conventional manner but after fifteen years they knew as much about one another factually as it was possible to know. It was over two months since Rose's last visit to the hairdresser's, so whatever was troubling Ann's daughter had occurred since then because, otherwise, Ann would have mentioned it. Doreen had expressed concern about Ann's granddaughter, Katy, who would, Rose calculated, be about six now. 'She's gone awful quiet lately, an' she's white as a sheet. Susan don't know what to do with her,' Doreen had said before going on to mention something about a doctor. Rose, her mind on something else at the time, had imagined that Katy had probably been suffering from one of the various childhood illnesses. But on reflection she realised that Doreen, who had brought up her own children, would not have expressed such concern if it had been as simple as that. Children's personalities changed in that way when something bad had happened to them. Rose could not imagine that the parents were involved. She had met them only once, which was not time enough to make a judgment, but Doreen knew them intimately and babysat for them on occasions. She trusted and liked them and always said that Katy was a 'treat' to look after; that she was a happy, friendly and obedient little girl. That was until recently. And Beth had gone missing. Could there possibly be a connection, she wondered. Adults were capable of doing terrible things to children, for their own gratuitous pleasure or for profit. However ridiculous he might think her suspicions to be, Rose wondered whether she ought to mention them to Jack.

She barely noticed the drive home because there were so many things to think about. Apart from Beth and Katy there was the problem of Christmas. Dad and I could have a quiet time alone, or I could invite Jack to liven us up a bit, she told herself. On the other hand, it might be painful for Arthur to see them together when he was so recently bereaved. The obvious answer was to ask him. And there was the usual dilemma of what to paint next. She had once vowed never to depict St Michael's Mount in any medium. It was the most drawn, painted and photographed scene in Cornwall, possibly in the whole of the West Country. Yet she had been on Marazion beach actually contemplating doing such a thing. She wondered if the mysteries of Cornwall had been at work, if something other than a desire to sketch the crashing seas had drawn here there on Tuesday, if some sort of premonition had motivated her. Myths and legends abounded and things happened which were seemingly inexplicable. That could have been one of them. Rose had developed the innate curiosity of the Cornish, the need to know everything about a person, but until that moment she had believed she had not picked up their superstitions. Driving along the A30 in the winter sunshine, she suddenly recalled one other winter afternoon. She had been sketching the Merry Maidens which lay just west of Lamorna in the hamlet of Boleigh; the name meaning a place of slaughter. There, so Laura had told her, Athelstan finally vanquished the Cornish in 936. Nearby, in a field, exists a circle of nineteen stones, said to be maidens who dared to dance on a Sunday to the tune of two pipers who were also turned to stone. The pipers stood some distance away. One of its attractions to Rose was that there was nothing else there at all. People could come and go as they chose. There was no entrance fee, no hut selling guidebooks or souvenirs, no refreshment van, not even a car park. It was simply those nineteen stones in a circle in a field. Nothing had altered in hundreds, possibly thousands of years.

That afternoon she had been the only person there and was therefore able to park in the limited space in the gateway by the stile. The sun had been slurring then, too, and she had almost finished the sketch when a cloud passed over the sun and she got the feeling she was not alone. When she looked around there was no one there and no other car had stopped. Her hair had prickled her scalp and she had had to stop herself from rushing back to the car. The moment soon passed but she had never forgotten it. Something indefinable had been at work.

By the time she got home the heating had come on, giving the house an even more welcoming feeling than usual. She hung up her jacket, removed the spool of film from the camera and replaced it with a new one. After a cup of tea she would finish the Morrab Garden palm, filling it in with colour.

While the kettle boiled she checked the answering machine. There were two messages. The first confirmed her booking for a table for three at seven at the Ocean Palace, the second was from Doreen. 'I need to see 'e, maid. It's not desperately urgent but I'd like a word. I could come over about four. My afternoon lady's in bed with flu so she's asked me just to do the downstairs today. I'll come anyway. If you're out, then you're out and if you're busy I'll push off again.'

Fat chance of that, Rose thought as she grinned. But she wanted to speak to Doreen so it might as well be today.

It was nearly half-past four when Doreen did arrive. She rapped on the glass of the kitchen door. Like Rose, and all her friends, she used the side entrance, off the drive where she parked, rather than walk around the narrow path to the front door which, through lack of use, had a tendency to stick.

Rose had finished in the attic. She had used a delicate wash for the palm with a background that merely suggested a blue sky and other foliage. She had also had time to develop the roll of film, which was now pegged up to dry. When Doreen knocked she was in the sitting-room studying one of her numerous plant books, determined to name the palm tree. She got up and went to let her in.

'If you're busy, I won't stop,' she said in her forthright way and, as always, without any form of salutation.

'I'm not, as it happens. I've done all I can for the moment.' There might even be time to make prints of the negatives before it was time to get ready to go out. David had converted part of the attic into a darkroom. There, Rose had taught herself the techniques of developing and printing and was now an expert in both sides of photography. She plugged in the kettle again. Doreen never refused the offer of a cup of tea, neither did she ever come empty-handed.

'I've brought you some of Cyril's brussel sprouts. Cambridge, I think he said the variety was called. Anyhow, they're early ones. We've had some, they be 'ansome. Cyril says the other ones aren't any good until later, after a bit of frost, not that we get much of that down here. And there's one of my lardy cakes. I know how you do love 'en.'

'Thank you.' Rose suppressed a smile. She rarely ate sweet things. What Doreen meant was that she would expect some, suitably warmed up and spread thickly with butter, with her tea.

'If you remember, I was talking about Susan Overton the other day. Well, little Katy isn't right yet, Rose. The doctor can't find anything the matter with her but even I can see the change in her. It's as if she isn't the same person any more.

I can't bear to see such a lovely family being so miserable. He's suffering, too, is Simon.'

'That's odd. I was going to ask you about them. I've been thinking so much about Beth and, well—' she stopped. It was impossible to mention to Doreen what she feared. It would probably do more harm than good.

But it was Doreen who voiced the fears. 'It's a wicked world, maid. I was wondering if Katy had been interfered with. Perhaps I'm as wicked as some of they out there for even thinking it, but it does happen. And, like you say, with that other small chiel missing it makes you wonder if there's some pervert around.'

Rose sighed. 'It had crossed my mind, too.' She placed the teapot on the kitchen table before removing the slices of lardy cake from the oven. Their appetising doughy smell rose from the heat. Doreen took a piece and smothered it in the rich, gold local butter Rose bought from a farm shop. It melted into the yeasty texture. She took a bite before speaking again. 'Is there anything we can do?'

'I really don't know. I mean, how does anyone go about finding out such things?'

The shrewd look which Doreen gave her told Rose what was coming next. 'You could mention it to Jack Pearce. Casual like, when you're talking about this, that and the third thing. He'll know if there's anyone like that around in the area. They have these lists now, I believe. Will you do that, maid? Will you ask him? Just a hint, like. He'll know what to do.'

'Okay.' She had half intended to do so anyway. Having told Doreen she would mention it, she had to keep her word.

Neither of them mentioned the subject again. They had said all that needed to be said. There was no point in dwelling on it. The conversation turned to more personal matters. Doreen's jaw dropped when Rose told her about Barry and Jenny. 'He's got hisself a woman? I'd never have believed it less'n you'd told me. Well I never. I always thought it was you he was after. Of course, I could see he had no chance. And there's no need to blush, girl, some things are obvious to others. Still, you've got Jack, and a good man he is, too. Don't ask me how you did it. You've got your looks and your figure, I'll grant you that, but I wish you'd take my advice and wear a frock more often, or, at least, a skirt. And I don't mean that skimpy little denim thing you wear in the summer. You'd never catch me in jeans or trousers.'

Rose glanced at the digital clock on the electric display unit of the gas cooker. Doreen could go on in this manner for hours. She needed to find a tactful way to ask her to leave. 'Actually, as soon as I've had a shower I will be changing into a dress. Jack's taking Dad and me out for dinner tonight. I'll mention what we've talked about if there's an appropriate moment.' Rose stood, pleased to note that Doreen had taken the hint and was already reaching for her padded jacket which was draped over the back of her chair.

'If he comes back for coffee make sure you give 'en some of my tardy cake,' were Doreen's parting words.

Geoff Carter was working late. There had been a leak in the roof of the annexe to his gallery where slates had come off in a gale and the builders had now left. They had needed fine weather in which to complete the job and the rain had held off until half an hour ago. The gallery itself was all chrome and glass and housed the works of local artists, including Rose Trevelyan. The annexe had yet to be modernised.

Twice married and divorced, Geoff admitted that he was a womaniser. When he first met Rose he had tried to get her into bed. Now he was thankful that she had not been interested. Their business relationship had developed into friendship as well, neither of which would have worked for long if sex had been involved because the affair would not have lasted.

Geoff had also persuaded Rose to take on the extra pupils who would not fit into the classes of another artist. These classes were held in the annexe; Rose's being held on a Wednesday night. That week's class had been cancelled because of the water dripping through the arched roof.

Satisfied that the place was habitable, Geoff went back into the gallery. He checked his appearance in one of the many mirrors, which were placed to convey a feeling of more space than there actually was. He was not vain but he knew he had worn well. His greying hair was worn longer than was usual for a man of his age. It was swept back and rested just below his collar. His brown eyes were full of humour and held an invitation to any woman who looked at him. Although he only sold paintings he encouraged young artists and dressed as they did. His vaguely bohemian appearance was the only hint of his great disappointment that he, himself, was a failed artist.

Right then he would have enjoyed Rose's

company. He didn't like the winter with long hours of darkness; she would have cheered him up. There was something soothing about her; something that suggested everything would be all right in time. He dialled her number and was pleased to hear her voice rather than a recorded one. 'Rose, the roof's finished. You can tell your lot that there'll be a class next week.'

'Good. Thanks for letting me know.' She had showered and washed her hair but was still wrapped in a towel.

'Can I take you out to celebrate?'

'Not tonight, Geoff, I'm already going out.'

Jack Pearce, the bastard, he thought with a touch of envy. An artist going out with a policeman, it didn't seem right somehow. 'Another time then?'

Rose detected the plaintiveness in his voice. Men were like children at times. 'Yes, another time.'

Geoff Carter switched on the alarm system and locked up. He was only vaguely aware of the car that was passing slowly down the lane but when he looked up he certainly noticed the attractive woman who was driving it, even though it was dark. She, in turn, noticed his undisguised gaze and, looking startled, accelerated down the street.

'I wouldn't say no to that one,' he muttered as he pocketed his keys and turned up the collar of his corduroy jacket against the rain.

Barry Rowe was preparing a meal in his flat above the shop. How right Rose had been about decorating it. For far too long he had let it go. And now it was a pleasure to cook in the completely refitted kitchen which a firm had come to measure up then planned to perfection for convenience and space.

Barry, whose culinary skills were limited, was grateful for the fact that Jenny was not a fussy eater. What he felt about her, he wasn't yet certain. It was too soon to tell where the relationship was going. What surprised him was that it had started at all.

Jenny had come into the shop looking for a birthday card knowing that everything he sold was in some way produced by local artists and craftsmen. Her granddaughter, baby Polly, had been with her at the time and had managed to tip her pram over and bang her head. Barry offered the use of his first aid box and it had started from there. He had met Rose, too, in his shop not long after she came to Cornwall, a short time after he had started the business when he had no idea if he could make a go of it.

He pushed his glasses into place and continued slicing chicken for the stir fry. The shop. How ironic that it was in the shop that he had also introduced Rose to David. It had taken him a long time to realise that Rose would never be his.

When David died, Barry had grieved for his friend but somewhere in his subconscious was a spark of hope that now she was free she might turn to him, might even need him. But it had become apparent that Rose didn't need anyone, not even Jack Pearce. What she felt for Jack was on some other level.

He heard Jenny's footsteps on the flight of metal stairs which led to the flat from the back of the building and went to let her in.

'It's started to rain,' she said as he took her damp mac.

'So I see.' He felt only the slightest pang that it was Jenny and not Rose with whom he would be sharing his meal.

'They still haven't found that little girl yet,' Jenny remarked as she took off her coat. 'God knows what the mother must be going through.'

Barry nodded. He couldn't even begin to imagine her feelings; all he knew was that Rose was involved and would remain so until the final outcome, whatever it might be. 'Would you like a drink? I think I've got almost everything.' He realised he had been influenced by Rose. At one time he would have gone to the pub if he fancied a pint.

'Wine for me, please.' Jenny sat down, smiling, as she watched him struggle with the corkscrew. He was a nice man and she thought she might already be halfway in love with him.

Arthur Forbes had bathed and shaved and taken trouble over his appearance despite what Rose had said. It would be far too easy to let himself go and he knew there were times when he was in danger of doing so now that there was no one living with him to care how he looked. Why should I worry when my daughter manages to be so popular when half the time she dresses like one of those New Age travellers, he thought with a wry smile.

The doorbell rang. Rose had a spare key to his house but she would never presume to use it unless there was an emergency. She would have hated anyone walking into her own home unannounced. 'Oh, very smart,' she said as she took in the tweed jacket, sharply pressed trousers and the turtleneck sweater.

Arthur held her shoulders and kissed her cheek.

Rose reminded him so much of Evelyn when she was younger.

'It's raining so Jack's brought the car.'

Arthur lived in a 1930s house in one of the side roads set back from the seafront. The houses, built on the side of a hill, were tiered and all had views of the bay. 'No point in moving to Penzance if I can't see the sea,' Arthur had commented at the time he was studying estate agents' details. It was too far from the restaurant to walk without getting soaked, especially as the wind had risen again and waves were sweeping over the Promenade. St Michael's Mount was obscured by the rain. In such weather even walking on the opposite side of the road was no guarantee of not getting hit by a wave, and the sand and weed that came with it.

Jack was waiting in the car. He didn't look very happy. Perhaps it was because of the missing child but Arthur thought it was more likely something his daughter had said or done. For once he was wrong.

Jack was thinking as he sat in the car. They had made the relevant enquiries and discovered that Sally Jones was not claiming benefits for herself and the child. So how was she managing to live? She had said that she had had no contact with

Poole for years. But Poole had been uncontactable that day so the matter would have to wait until the morning. Jack was determined to relax and enjoy the evening. No one could work properly when stressed.

According to Poole, Sally had convinced him it was better for them all if Beth never knew him. And if Sally met someone else Beth could treat that man as her father. 'It nearly broke my heart but I began to see that she might be right,' he had continued. Were those sentiments genuine or were they just an excuse for Poole to start a new life unencumbered by a child? And what to do about Sally Jones? Perhaps there was some private income they did not know about. There were other things on his mind, too, but they could wait. He didn't want to spoil the evening for Rose and Arthur.

Arthur and Rose hurried towards the car and got in. Jack drove off. 'We've time for a quick drink,' he said once he'd manoeuvred the car into a space in one of the side roads near the restaurant.

'Suits me,' Arthur said, willing to go along with whatever they wanted.

They walked the short distance to the Dock, a pub Arthur had not been in before. It was busier than they had anticipated, but they wouldn't be there for very long.

'Do you both know everyone in Penzance and Newlyn?' Arthur asked when Rose and Jack had greeted several people. Some they knew jointly, others, individually.

'It sometimes seems like it. You will, too, Dad, in a little while.' She hoped she was right. She had already found someone to introduce him to the captain of one of the bowls clubs, which he hoped to join.

Several more customers arrived. They drank up quickly and went back out into the rain but the Ocean Palace was almost next door. They sat by the fire whilst they ordered their food from the extensive menu. Then they were taken to their table which was up a short flight of stairs. The interior was on several levels and the decor was reminiscent of a Spanish restaurant rather than a Chinese one.

Not once throughout the meal did Jack refer to Beth although Rose guessed she was uppermost in his mind. And he had not relaxed. She could see by the way in which he held himself and the grim expression on his face when he was unaware he was being observed.

'That was delicious, Jack. Many thanks,'

Arthur said as he wiped his mouth with his serviette. 'My turn next time.'

Rose smiled at him. Her father had a dread of not paying his way. 'If you're ready I'll run you both home.'

The rain had eased to a steady drizzle and the tide was ebbing. The waves were less fierce but it was not a night to be at sea.

They dropped Arthur outside his house and Jack made sure he was safely in with the lights on before carrying on to Newlyn.

'Do you want some coffee? Only if you do, Doreen insists you have a piece of her lardy cake.' Because Jack was driving Rose and her father had drunk most of the wine. 'Or if you prefer, I've got some of your favourite whisky.'

By offering him spirits he knew she was also offering him a bed for the night. 'Whisky sounds wonderful.'

Jack parked behind Rose's car in the drive whilst she unlocked the kitchen door. It was still quite early, not long after nine o'clock; there would be time to talk. Rose could sense that that was what Jack wanted but had refrained from doing so over the meal.

They took their drinks into the sitting-room and sat either side of the fireplace. Rose sat in the armchair David had always occupied. She had done so since shortly after he died. She wondered if it was a subconscious act to prevent anyone else from doing so. Despite the wind and rain it was still quite mild. The fire remained unlit as the central heating was on and it would have been overpoweringly warm. The table lamps, with their pink shades, gave the room a cosy glow. Because of the pattern of raindrops on the window the view was obscured, no more than a blur of lights and a glint of sea. St Michael's Mount had totally disappeared.

'Sally Jones has not been claiming benefits,' Jack began without preamble. No one else was aware of this yet. He wasn't sure how to deal with this aspect of the case and he wanted Rose's opinion before he made up his mind.

'I did wonder about that. She seemed very evasive when she spoke of Michael.'

'We haven't been able to get in touch with him today, he's away on a longer trip.'

Rose placed her wine glass on the small table at her side, smoothed down the skirt of her blue wool dress then lit a cigarette. She thought she knew what was going through his mind. 'Do you think she's harmed her own child?'

'It's always a possibility. Single mothers who

can't cope have been known to do so. And I know, before you say it, you saw a man take Beth from the beach, but that could have been prearranged.'

'Well, then he's still as guilty as she is.'

'Quite.'

'So what're you going to do?'

Jack shrugged as he swirled the whisky in his glass. 'I haven't a clue. What would you do?'

Rose laughed in astonishment at the question before she considered her answer. 'I think I'd wait until I knew one way or another about Beth. Wherever she's getting the money Sally's got enough to deal with at the moment.'

'That was my gut feeling. I'm glad you agree with me.'

'There are times, Inspector Pearce, when we do think along the same lines. Still, none of it feels right to you, does it?'

'How did you know that?'

'Because that's how I feel. When I was at Carol's I got the feeling that there was a lot more going on than anyone's saying.' She regretted the words as soon as she had spoken them. Jack hadn't known about that visit.

'You went to see the sister? My God, Rose, I don't know how you had the nerve. You don't even know her.'

'I had met her once, actually,' she replied defensively. 'And it was Norma's idea, not mine.'

'Norma, as in Mrs Penhalligon, I take it. How on earth do you manage to get yourself involved with strangers so very quickly? No, don't answer. I'd rather not know.' He wasn't angry, not this time. In fact, there was always the chance that Rose would find out something they might miss. Not because of incompetence or stupidity but because people quickly looked upon Rose as a confidante. 'Just be careful, my girl, that's all.'

'Yes, dear. Whatever you say.'

Jack grinned at her. Rose was stubborn; she would not be careful. However, he was beginning to relax and Rose looked lovely that evening. More so than usual, he supposed, because she was not clad in her paint splattered jeans. He yawned and swallowed the rest of his whisky.

Rose could see he was ready for bed.

Marcus Holt paced the floor of the lounge of his small terraced house. It had been purchased with his share of the proceeds of his divorce five years previously. His wife had moved back to London to be near her family.

Marcus had taken a week off from work. Holiday he was long overdue from the electrical retail firm for whom he worked; although he could hardly have called it a holiday. Carol and her problems were too much on his mind.

He had met her in the store when she had come in to buy some electrical equipment. He couldn't recall what it was but he had been infatuated with her from the start. Her curves were all in the right places and she had a mass of reddish brown hair. There was an earthiness about her he couldn't resist, even when she had told him she was married. She was, in fact, the complete opposite of Sheila, his thin, blonde ex-wife.

The sex was terrific, although there had been far less of it recently. He had also noticed a change in Carol's attitude towards him. Until the past few days he had not doubted that she would leave John and move in with him. Now he had a strong impression that he had been carefully manipulated and once his usefulness had expired she would leave him. But how can she leave me when she's never really been with me? he asked himself.

I'll really have to give her an ultimatum, he realised as he wondered just how much of what she had told him was true. Sunday evening would be the limit, it would have to be. That was also when her children returned from their grandparents' house ready to return to school. They had been given a couple of days off because of their distress at what had happened to their cousin. Their headmistress thought that remaining with their grandparents might provide a distraction. She was fully aware of how quickly children forgot things.

He had been an utter fool. Carol must now accept the consequences of her actions, just as he would have to do.

There was an alternative but Marcus Holt did not have the courage for that. It had taken him far too long to acknowledge the danger of becoming involved with a woman like Carol.

Michael Poole finished his day's work then returned to his cottage in Looe where he packed an overnight bag. There was no way he could stay away from Sally any longer. And he was almost physically sick with worry over Beth. He had really believed it was better to go along with what Sally had said, but the reality of not seeing his daughter – of perhaps never seeing her again – was a lot harder to deal with than he had imagined.

He hung up his suit, changed into more casual clothes and ran a comb through his short, fair hair. He locked up the cottage and began his drive to Marazion.

It was Carol who had given him Sally's address. 'She doesn't want you to know where she is,' she had said in that bitter tone of voice he had come to accept.

'For heaven's sake, Carol, Beth's missing, my daughter's missing, things are different now.' Speaking the words made them real and had brought tears to his eyes. 'Sally needs all the support she can get right now. You, as a mother, must realise that.'

Reluctantly, Carol had given him directions.

Michael had no idea what sort of a reception he would receive, neither did he care. He just had to be there and he knew he was doing the right thing.

The Friday night traffic began to thin out and he reached Marazion a little after seven thirty. He had driven in the dark and it had rained all the way down and continued to do so. The road was black and shiny beneath the streetlamps and the wipers swished back and forth soporifically. The chill damp air revived him after the stuffiness of the car when he finally found somewhere to park.

Lights shone from the windows of pubs and many of the cottages that lined the streets but there were few pedestrians around. The rhythmic sound of waves breaking echoed in the stillness and he could smell the salt from the spray. He stopped briefly to look at the Mount, visible from where he stood because it was close to the land. It rose majestically out of the water.

Wandering through the narrow streets he eventually found the house he was looking for. Lights shone from the windows on both stories. There were two bells. He pressed the one marked Jones.

It was several minutes before he heard movement from inside the house. The door opened and he stood face to face with Sally's mother. 'Hello, Alice,' he said, pleased to have met with her first because she had always liked and approved of him and had been disappointed when Sally had decided to end their relationship. Even now, he had no idea why she had done so.

'I'm so glad you're here. You'd better come in.'

Michael followed her up the stairs, dreading the pain he was about to witness.

CHAPTER SIX

For most of the week the Tesco store on the outskirts of Penzance remained open twenty-four hours a day. It was where Geoff Carter did his shopping. Never able to sleep for more than four or five hours a night he enjoyed the odd sensation of buying his groceries along with shift workers and other insomniacs when everyone else was asleep. However, the disadvantage was that the liquor department had to abide by the licensing laws and the counters selling fresh meat, fish and cheeses were also closed at night.

Wandering along the aisles with a trolley he passed several staff who were restocking the shelves. And then, to his amazement, as he rounded a corner he came face to face with the woman he was sure he had seen driving past the gallery earlier that evening. Some might have called this coincidence. Geoff Carter, who had previously noticed how attractive she was, decided it had to be fate. 'Hello,' he said brazenly as, without appearing to do so, he took in her curves, her slim legs in tight fitting jeans and her hair, which glinted beneath the fluorescent lights. She looked wholesome and clean and it seemed appropriate that the aroma of fresh bread coming from the shelves where they stood should be enveloping them. As he stepped closer he recognised the light floral scent she wore. His first wife had used it, too. 'I think I might have seen you earlier, in Penzance.'

Her face reddened. 'Oh, I . . . yes. I was visiting my children.'

'Don't they live with you?' Her unexpected answer had taken him by surprise. He had not intended to be so abrupt but it was certainly an odd thing to admit to a stranger. When he first saw her he had imagined she would probably ignore his greeting and walk on past.

'Yes, of course they do. It's just that they're staying with their grandparents for a day or two. They're coming home on Sunday. I've had some problems, I needed a break, you see.'

I should've kept my mouth shut, he thought. There were tears in the woman's eyes. He did not wish to become involved with a neurotic. On the other hand, her vulnerability touched him, and she was certainly a looker. 'Can't your husband help you out?' he asked as casually as possible because he was actually trying to ascertain if there was a husband.

She shook her head. 'He's away at the moment. Look, I must get on.' She realised the mistake in continuing the conversation and having admitted so much, but he had taken her by surprise.

'If there's anything I can do to help, I'll be only too pleased. My name's Geoff Carter, by the way.'

'I'm Carol, Carol Harte.' Then the tears started in earnest. They ran down her face whilst she fumbled in her bag for a handkerchief. 'I'm so sorry. I really don't know what's the matter with me.'

'Why don't we give up on the shopping? If you're not up to it I can run you home and you can collect your car another time.' He now felt genuinely sorry for her; vulnerability in females appealed to him as much as their faces and figures.

'I'll be fine to drive, really.'

She looked down at the floor and hesitated before walking away. It was all the encouragement he needed.

'Then let me follow you, just to make sure you're all right. I promise you I won't get out of the car. You'll be quite safe.' He reached into his jacket pocket and produced one of his business cards which gave his name and the address and telephone number of the gallery. 'That's who I am. I won't be going anywhere. Now that you know exactly where I can be found, I hope that you'll trust me.'

Carol, who had not been to visit her children who would, in any case, have been asleep by then, had been to see Marcus. She was hardly inside the door when he had delivered his ultimatum. She had no idea what to do or to whom she could turn. Now, out of the blue, this man who claimed to have seen her in Penzance was taking an interest. Talking to a stranger might help, not that she could confide in him, but it might help ease some of the tension. Only because she didn't want to be alone did she take him up on his invitation. 'Thank you, I'd be grateful if you would. I live the other side of Marazion, though. I'm sure it'll be out of your way'

'It's no problem. Come on, let's go.'

They paid for their groceries and left the store.

There were few cars in the car park and the sodium lamps distorted the colours of those they could see. Geoff escorted Carol to her white Citroen, returned to his own vehicle, the van he used for transporting works of art, then followed her out on to the main road. She was nervous, he realised that by the way in which she kept glancing in her rear view mirror. But whether that was because she had regretted agreeing to his following her, or if it was simply to check he was still there, he didn't know.

Jack's mobile phone woke them. He had closed his eyes the moment he got into bed the previous night but felt no better for eight hours' sleep. 'Hello,' he snapped once he'd grabbed it from the bedside table, not fully aware of where he was. Not his own bedroom, that was certain. It was still dark but he gradually made out the shapes of Rose's familiar furniture. He was in her wooden bed in the plainly but pleasingly decorated room, which resembled that of a farmhouse bedroom rather than a fisherman's cottage. 'In that case my hands are tied. I'll be in as soon as possible,' he said after he had listened to the caller for a minute or two.

'What is it, Jack?' Rose had switched on her bedside light and was sitting up in bed.

'They've called off the bloody search. Orders from above. Enough time and money's been wasted, apparently. How can you waste those things when a child's life is involved?' The understanding had been the search would continue at daylight that morning. But deep down he feared no search would ever bring Beth back. Experts as well as local police and volunteers had covered miles of ground around the Marazion area. The roadblocks had been in place as quickly as possible and there was no way in which every inch of the county could be searched. Even then, if her body had been dumped, it could have been at sea or in a cave or one of the numerous old mine workings where it would never be found. He had seen this coming but known he was unable to prevent it. Orders from above could not be disobeyed.

'Have a quick shower, I'll make you some coffee,' Rose told him as she got out of bed and pulled on her towelling robe. It smelt of the softener she used in the wash. 'And if there's time, there's something I should mention. I meant to discuss it with you last night but I could see you were too tired. It'll only take a minute, I promise, but I think you ought to know before you go in.'

Jesus Christ, he thought as he went along the landing to the bathroom. What has the woman been up to now?

Rose knew that Jack wouldn't want to wait for the filter coffee to run through the machine so she spooned instant into two mugs and tried to think of a way to phrase what she wanted to say to him.

The kettle boiled. She poured water over the granules, added sugar to Jack's mug then carried the two black coffees into the sitting-room. The shower was still running. Jack's coffee would have a chance to cool a little.

It was a few minutes past seven. So far west the day broke later than in other parts of the country but there was the advantage of lighter evenings. In the height of the summer daylight could last until as late as ten thirty or even eleven.

That morning, in the winter predawn, the sea was a steely grey; the land stretching around the bay a semicircle of blackish humps outlined against the sky. The familiar outline of St Michael's Mount loomed darkly against the skyline. Over the land was a band of red, filtering upwards to pink before turning the streaky clouds a brilliant orange.

Rose held her breath. Every dawn and every sunset was different. The colours changed so rapidly they would be impossible to paint. Already the sky was lightening; blackbird egg blue in the west, pearly white to the east. The sun was rising. Nature was putting on a good show.

'What did you want to tell me?'

She turned. Jack stood in the doorway, she had not heard him approach. He crossed the sitting-room and joined her by the window where he picked up his mug from the sill. The steam had left a circle of condensation on a pane of glass. Rose watched him take a sip of coffee. His dark hair curled damply and he smelt of her shower gel. There were dark smudges beneath his eyes but he was still handsome and she would very much like to have taken him back upstairs. She inhaled deeply before speaking. To Jack this was a sure sign that she was nervous. 'To put it bluntly, Doreen is worried about the daughter of someone she knows. She's only six and her personality has changed completely.'

'So?'

'So, Jack, we wondered if there might be a connection with whatever's happened to Beth.'

'You're really not making much sense, Rose.'

I'm not, she realised, and I really should

have thought all this through properly before mentioning it. 'Little girls, that's what I'm talking about. For instance, have there been any recent cases of child abuse? Look, I know you can't answer that, but you hear of these paedophile rings and, as Doreen pointed out, these offenders are on some sort of list nowadays.'

'Doreen Clarke is a terrible gossip, as you well know. I imagined you'd know better than to listen to her.'

'I thought you liked her.' Rose was indignant.

'Since when has that had anything to do with it? You know I like her but that doesn't alter the fact that she gossips.' He hadn't meant to snap but Rose had touched a nerve. There had been a recent case of sexual abuse involving an eight-year-old girl. Whoever was responsible had not yet been caught. The girl in question, Mandy, had been on her way home from school when she had quarrelled with the friend she was walking with. Mandy had lagged behind letting Linda walk on alone. When Linda finally looked back Mandy was nowhere to be seen. 'I thought she was hiding, to pay me back,' Linda had told the female officer who was following up on what Mandy had told her. But Mandy had been dragged into a car not far from her school. It had happened so quickly and, as unlikely as it seemed at that time of the day, there had been no witnesses. However, unlike in Beth's case, Mandy had been shoved out of the car and left by the roadside in a quiet lane where, some minutes later, a passing motorist had found her in a shocked and disorientated state. Sensibly, he had rung the police from his mobile phone rather than offer her a lift. And he waited until we arrived, Jack recalled. The man had also given a voluntary statement. Had he been the abuser he would not have done either. No one would ever know the extent of the mental damage it might have caused Mandy.

She had said the man was big, but to a child of that age any man would probably seem so. And dark haired. Rose had seen a dark haired man take Beth from the beach.

Jack sighed. 'What exactly do you expect me to do? I can hardly knock on the door and ask these people if someone is abusing their daughter. What's their name, anyway?'

'They're called Overton. The daughter's name is Katy. I know the grandmother, Ann. She usually cuts my hair. I've met Susan and Simon, they're the parents, but only once.'

I should have guessed Rose would have to know one or other of the parties involved, he thought. 'Do you believe Doreen, or is it just a case of her imagination working overtime?'

'I believe her, Jack. She seems genuinely upset.'

'Okay. If there's any way in which I can make discreet enquiries I'll do so. Now, I really must go.' He handed her his mug which was still half full of coffee before he hurried out of the house.

Daylight had arrived but the spectacular dawn had held a false promise. Clouds were beginning to bank up over the land and within minutes it started to rain. Apart from the fishing forecasts, no one bothered with what the meteorologists had to say. On the narrow peninsular, surrounded as it was by water, it was impossible to predict with any accuracy forthcoming weather. Sunshine could give way to rain in seconds or a storm could pass over abruptly leaving a clear blue sky.

Rose went to the kitchen and checked the fridge. It was almost empty, some shopping needed to be done. While the kettle boiled for a second mug of coffee she peeled an orange and broke it into segments, enjoying the tangy smell of the rind. Juice ran over her fingers. She rinsed them at the sink then began to eat. The telephone interrupted her.

It was Geoff Carter. For a moment Rose expected another invitation for dinner.

'I'm at the gallery. The post is here and I thought you'd like to know that a cheque has arrived. They've finally sorted out the finances of your last exhibition and sent me the balance. Well, you know how it is, they keep the money for as long as possible before they deduct their exorbitant commission and pay the poor artists.'

'I know that, Geoff. And you, as a gallery owner yourself, are no less to blame.'

'Ah, how well you know me, Rose, dear. But if you want your money you'd better be nice to me.'

'Naturally. But then I'm nice to everyone. I'll come in this morning to collect my dues. Have the cheque ready, it's going straight into the building society.'

'The building society? You're obviously making more money than you need to live on. Something's definitely wrong with the world when an artist can do that. In the circumstances I think you should marry me.'

'Then think on, Geoffrey Carter. You are definitely not husband material. Anyway, it's only just gone eight. What on earth are you doing at the gallery so early?'

'The usual. A touch of insomnia. In fact . . .'

'In fact, what?'

'Oh, it's nothing really. It can wait. I'll tell you

about it over coffee. You'll have time for one, won't you, before you pop in to the Bristol & West?'

'Yes. They're open until twelve on Saturdays.' Rose was intrigued. Geoff's bantering tone had turned serious.

By the time she had showered and dressed, made the bed and written out a shopping list, it was pouring with rain. The list was quite long. This year she was going to make a Christmas cake as she knew how much her father enjoyed it, although she had left it a little late. In previous years, when David was alive she had baked it in September then added brandy at regular intervals via holes made with a knitting needle; the result a delicious moistness.

She pulled on her mac, picked up her car keys and went out into the rain. Water dripped from the guttering where dead leaves had gathered again. She would ask Trevor if he'd mind removing them. Instead of the sea she could smell the damp soil and vegetation and, as her legs brushed against them, the strong scent of the pelargonium leaves, which managed to survive the winters out of doors because of the mildness of the climate.

Geoff Carter's place first, she decided as she

started the engine. That way her cheque would be safely in the building society by lunchtime. No longer with cause to, Rose still worried about money. David had left her well provided for and the mortgage had been paid up upon his death. There were his pensions and what she earned from her work, but two days' interest was two days' interest as far as Rose was concerned so why wait until Monday to pay in her money?

Carol Harte slept very little on Friday night. Dreams turned into nightmares and when she woke for the second time her nightdress was damp with sweat. Life, she realised as she switched on the bedside lamp, had turned into one huge nightmare. One of her own making. She went downstairs to make tea knowing that she would not sleep again. Her reflection in the blackness of the kitchen window showed a pale faced, tired looking woman who could look so attractive when she was happy. When was that? When was the last time I was happy? she asked herself. She had expected to be the one to offer an ultimatum to Marcus, not to be on the receiving end of one. The tables had turned. She had lost control of the situation. She might well have lost everything. And as for her actions later last night, how could she have been so very stupid? I didn't tell him anything, I didn't tell him anything that mattered, she repeated, hoping that by doing so it would become the truth. But she suspected that Geoff Carter would not forget what she had told him.

The kettle began to boil. She placed a teabag in a cup, poured on water and added milk. Beneath the fluorescent light strip the tea seemed to have a filmy surface. She tipped it down the sink and made coffee instead.

Fifteen minutes later the sheets and duvet cover between which she had tossed in the night were churning around in the washing machine and clean linen was already on the bed.

Perhaps later, at a more sociable time, she would go and see Sally again. It just might help her to get her thoughts in order. There would be no need to concentrate on the conversation, she knew exactly how it would go, for what else would they talk about but Beth? And maybe by talking about her Carol would find a solution to her own problems.

Sally had only slept fitfully, not the sleep of exhaustion, which would have done her good. She had reached the stage of numbness when whatever news she received would have no impact. Lack of food wasn't helping, either, but

124

the thought of eating made her gag. Beth was dead. How soon would her body be recovered and someone came to break the news?

First thing on Saturday morning, at her mother's insistence, Sally went to have a bath, wash her hair and change out of the clothes she had worn for the past two days.

'It'll do you good,' Alice Jones had said. 'And you don't want to let Michael see you looking like that.'

Her mother was right. It would be added fuel to his belief that she was not a fit mother if she was unwashed when he arrived.

Alice had no idea how to console her daughter, how anyone could. All she knew was her own pain. How much greater must Sally's be. She made a halfhearted effort to tidy up although, in the circumstances, it seemed such a futile thing to do. It was raining hard but unseasonably mild. She opened the windows wide and let the fresh air blow through the flat, ridding it of the stale smell of cigarettes and the mugginess of the fire which had been left on all the time because Sally felt chilled to the bone.

Sally sat on the lid of the toilet while the water ran and steam filled the bathroom. What a shock it had been to see Michael last night. For one fleeting second she thought he had come to say that Beth was alive and well. But that couldn't be so, not now.

She had always believed Michael to be a decent, honourable man, his only fault his utter devotion to her, his continual pressing her to get married. She had wondered if his attempt to gain custody had been another way of trying to force her to stay with him. But now she knew the unspeakable truth.

Sally had wanted a child more than she had wanted marriage, and despite what she had said she did not want that daily journey from Looe to Plymouth where she had worked as a floor manager in a department store. Having Beth had put an end to that. Hot tears burnt her eyes. They ran down her face and fell into the bath water as she sat, head in her hands, elbows on the edge of the bath and sobbed until her throat ached and there were no more tears left to shed. The running water drowned the sounds. If I'd stayed with Michael this wouldn't have happened, she thought. It's my fault. Everything that's happened is my fault.

She peeled off the jeans, sweatshirt and underwear she had lived in for the past two days and threw them into the laundry basket. With trembling legs she stepped over the side of the bath and sank beneath the hot water. It lapped comfortingly around her body and soaked her short hair as she lay back. With her eyes closed she thought how sensitive and calm Michael had been last night.

'I just want to help. I'll do anything in the world if it means getting Beth back,' he had said quietly. 'I'll find somewhere to stay. The job doesn't matter. My boss will either understand or he won't. I should have come sooner, I know that now, but the police advised me not to.'

Alice and Sally were aware that the police would not have given him the address without asking Sally's permission. He must have obtained it from Carol. Alice, who knew her older daughter far better than Carol would ever have guessed, wondered exactly what her motives had been. Time, no doubt, would tell.

'If it's all right, I'll come back in the morning,' Michael had said. 'There must be something I can do.'

Sally was grateful for those words but hated to admit that Michael's presence was reassuring. She was glad he was returning today. The police were in touch with them at regular intervals, telephoning far too frequently, Sally thought, because each time the phone rang it raised her hopes and made her think she might have got it all wrong.

As she was dressing she heard voices. One was that of her mother, the second was also female. Not Michael, then, so it had to be Carol.

* * *

Jack logged on to the computer and checked all the known paedophiles in the area. There were remarkably few. However, no one could know what happened in the privacy of other people's homes or how many children remained silent. But this, Jack thought, is not the case here. It was not a question of abuse by a member of the family. Mandy had been taken from the street by a stranger, subjected to sexual assault, although, thank God, not full penetration, and had then been dumped. She was adamant that she had never seen the man before even though her description of him was vague. That was to be expected. She must have been terrified as well as full of revulsion at what was happening to her

Beth, too, had been snatched, apparently at random. In neither instance did the profile match anyone on their files, but nor did Jack have any idea whether the same person was responsible for both crimes.

And now there was Rose's concern about little Katy Overton. From what she had said it seemed if anything was going on it was down to one or other of the parents.

'But what can I do about it?' he asked himself aloud as he paced his office, his hands in his jacket pockets. 'How can we possibly interfere without the slightest bit of evidence?'

I've got it, he thought. He would send someone around to the local schools to talk to the children under the guise of crime prevention, offering sound advice such as never, ever getting into a stranger's car. Child helpline numbers could be left and the children encouraged to talk to their teachers if they had any worries or problems.

The constable, if picked carefully, could tactfully probe the teaching staff to see if they had any fears for any of their pupils or if any of them had developed behavioural problems. But he or she would have to probe very tactfully. There had been as many, if not more, cases of overzealous authoritarian individuals who had caused children to be taken from safe, loving homes than those abused ones who slipped through the system. Yes, he would do it. Surely one officer could be spared for a day. But it was Saturday, he could not put the plan into action until Monday. Jack left his office and went to find the uniformed colleague who would be able to recommend the right man or woman for the job.

CHAPTER SEVEN

Susan Overton enjoyed the comfort of the feel of her daughter's small hand in her own as they walked towards the supermarket in Hayle. There were only a couple of items she needed because she always did the bulk of the shopping when Katy was at school. They were wrapped up against the rain but it had not been worth getting out the car for such a short journey and neither of them had been out of the house yet that day.

To their left was the River Hayle, its surface dotted with small concentric circles as the rain hit the slowly ebbing water. Huddled along its banks were a variety of ducks.

'Look,' Katy said, 'an egret.'

Susan smiled. Katy had spoken with a touch of her old enthusiasm. 'So it is.' Once rare, there were now many to be seen in the area. The heron-like snow-white bird stood, shoulders hunched, in the reeds, its distinctive yellow feet hidden. There was nothing wrong with Katy's memory. It was some months now since Susan had told her the name of the bird.

They reached the shelter of the store, which, being a Saturday morning, was busy. The warmth from the overhead heating immediately inside the doorway was welcome. Susan picked up a basket and still holding Katy's hand, began to search the shelves for the items she required.

'Would you like some sweets?' she asked when they reached the checkout queue. 'Katy? Did you hear what I said?'

Katy nodded as she looked down at her shoes. 'Yes, please.'

Why the hesitation, Susan wondered. Had the doctor been wrong? Maybe her daughter really was suffering from stomach ache but didn't want to say. And recently she had only picked at her food. Having examined Katy thoroughly he could find nothing physically wrong. 'You choose something, darling. It's our turn to pay next.'

Katy looked at the shelves where the sweets

and chocolates were displayed temptingly at children's eye level next to the tills. She wanted something that would last, that she could sit and enjoy throughout the whole of the video she was to be allowed to watch that afternoon. It was a rare treat. At the weekend they usually went out as a family but her father had some extra paperwork to catch up on that day. Tomorrow they were going to Paradise Park, which was no distance away. Katy loved the exotic birds with their raucous cries. And then it would be Monday, only she wouldn't think about that yet.

Susan noticed that Katy had chosen a packet of boiled sweets instead of her favourite chocolate, but said nothing. The doctor had suggested that she was going through a phase; maybe her tastes were changing accordingly.

Later that afternoon, when Simon had finished his paperwork, he went to see if there was a chance of a cup of tea. Susan was not in the kitchen where she had been ironing, but was standing in the doorway of the lounge watching their daughter who was gazing raptly at the cartoon video on the television screen. The sweets were beside her on the settee.

'She's smiling,' Susan whispered.

'So I see.' Simon took his wife's hand and they

went to the kitchen, leaving Katy to enjoy the rest of the video.

It was the first time for weeks they had seen her enjoy anything. Perhaps whatever had been troubling her had been forgotten. 'Shall I help you with the meal?' Simon asked.

'That'd be nice.' Susan smiled and tried to put all thoughts of Simon's brother out of her mind. How could she possibly accuse him of what she suspected? But it was the only alternative explanation she could think of.

The gallery was open and brightly lit against the gloom of the morning, but also to attract customers in. Concealed spotlights picked out Geoff's favourite pieces. Although he dealt predominantly with paintings in various media there were also a few ceramics and some bronze sculptures.

Rose pushed open the door and walked into the comparative warmth of the building with its familiar smells: hessian, which lined the walls, coffee, which was always on the go as Geoff believed in looking after his customers, and the French cigarettes which he smoked in the small kitchen at the back of the gallery.

Geoff was seated behind the antique desk,

which served as a counter, his legs crossed, as he leafed through an old exhibition brochure. The artist he had once encouraged had gone on to big things; not that Geoff particularly liked his present work. It smacked of Damien Hirst and Martin Creed; the Emperor's New Clothes school of art, he, and others, called it cynically. How anyone could be awarded a large sum of money for turning a light switch on and off was beyond him.

He looked up and grinned when the buzzer on the door sounded and he saw Rose standing there, her mac spotted with rain. Rose, he believed, would also make it despite her more traditional style of painting. 'I was expecting you sooner,' he said as he stood to greet her. 'I thought you couldn't wait to get your grubby little hands on the cheque.'

'I can't. Where is it?'

He opened a desk drawer and took it out then waved it before her. 'The ink's hardly dry, my child. Here, take it, you've earned it, after all. Have you time for a coffee?'

'Yes, please.' Geoff's coffee was always excellent. He bought the beans and ground them himself

Rose knew how much the cheque would be

made out for but she examined it just the same as if to reassure herself that her work really was worth the four-figure sum written on it. All of her paintings had finally sold by the time the exhibition had come to a close. However, as Geoff had pointed out she had had to wait until it was finally over before she was paid a penny. Now she could certainly make it a good Christmas for her father.

She would be seeing him later as he had invited her for dinner. I must remember to ask him if he'd mind Jack being there, she thought. And Laura had rung to say she might call in sometime during the afternoon. Formality between the two friends had not existed for many years.

Geoff returned from the kitchen and placed two bone china cups and saucers on his desk before pulling up a second chair for Rose.

'What were you going to tell me?' she asked, suddenly recalling their earlier telephone conversation.

'I was hoping you'd forgotten.' He leant back in his swivel chair and folded his arms. 'I'm not altogether certain I should be telling you at all.'

'You know perfectly well it won't go any further.'

He did. Rose was totally trustworthy. 'Well, I

had a rather interesting encounter last night. In Tesco's, as it happens.'

Rose smiled. 'There you are. I knew supermarkets had to have something going for them.' She rarely used them. She was well supplied with fish, plus the vegetables from Cyril Clarke and she preferred to support the local shops. There were numerous bakers and greengrocers in Penzance and two butchers' in Newlyn, both of which sold meat from the animals the owners reared themselves. 'Well, go on then, don't keep me in suspense.'

Geoff stroked his chin. He hoped Rose wasn't going to think he was merely boasting. 'I was finishing off in here late last night, locking up, actually, when I noticed this woman drive past.'

'Noticed? I take it she was good-looking then.' Rose knew she would have had to have been for Geoff to have noticed her.

'Indeed. Extremely. Anyway, I decided to get the shopping out of the way and there she was again. I said hello and we got talking. She'd been to see her children, apparently.' He related the rest of their initial conversation.

'She let you follow her home? That was a bit risky, wasn't it? I mean, at that time of night and after she'd told you her husband and children were away. Don't look at me like that, I didn't mean you were a risk, I simply meant it from her point of view.'

'I'd given her one of my business cards.'

'Oh, and that proves you're no sort of danger, I suppose. Either the woman's a fool or she was in a worst state than you imagined.'

'It was the latter but I certainly didn't underestimate the state of her mind. Well, I followed her out to this bungalow somewhere the other side of Marazion. Despite how upset she was, she obviously isn't a fearful woman because the place was in the middle of nowhere and although she's there on her own at the moment there wasn't a light on anywhere. It was pitch black out there.'

Warning bells were sounding in Rose's head at the same instant as the buzzer on the door heralded the entrance of a prospective customer.

Geoff stood up, smiling, and went to offer his assistance. 'Don't go,' he said to Rose. 'Help yourself to another coffee.'

She shook her head. She didn't want another coffee, she wanted to hear the rest of Geoff's story.

Geoff spent almost fifteen minutes with the customer who left without buying anything. He shrugged as the door closed behind her. 'You can't win them all. She wasn't even interested in either of yours. I've only got two left, by the way. Are there any more in the pipeline?'

'Yes, an oil that's almost ready and another one that shouldn't take me more than a week or two. Come on, sit down and tell me the rest of it.'

He knew she would not be satisfied until she had been told all the events of the previous night and regretted having mentioned it over the telephone. 'When we first arrived there I wasn't sure whether or not to get out of the car. I didn't want to alarm her but I didn't like the idea of her in the darkness, trying to get into her house. However, she surprised me by coming over and asking if I wanted to come in for a coffee.'

'And I bet you thought your luck was in.' He never gives up, she thought as she pushed back some tendrils of hair which had come loose from the clip at the nape of her neck.

'Actually, no. I could tell by her manner it wasn't that. And she'd been in tears in Tesco's. I realised she just needed someone to talk to. Honestly, Rose, you'd have done the same if you'd seen how sad and vulnerable she looked.'

Rose believed him even though it was a side of Geoff Carter she had never seen before.

'We went inside and she made us coffee and then she told me about the terrible mess she's in, a mess she doesn't know how to extract herself from. She admitted that she's never been sure if she loves her husband, that she married him on the rebound and that recently she's been seeing another man.' He stopped, as if a memory had come to the surface. 'I don't usually notice such things but the place was spotless. Mind you, it reeked of bleach, which was a bit off-putting when you're drinking coffee.'

Rose was astonished on two counts. People confided in her but not usually to the extent that this woman had confided in Geoff upon a first meeting. 'I suppose she can't decide between the husband and lover.' Loyalty ought to come first but if she were desperately miserable and remained at home, no one would gain. Misery, she knew, bred more misery. The second thing which had struck her and which she had at first believed to be no more than coincidence, now seemed certain. But she had to ask. 'Geoff, this woman's name wasn't Carol Harte, by any chance?'

It was his turn to be surprised. It showed in his eyes. 'How on earth did you know that? Don't tell me you've turned into some kind of Cornish soothsayer.'

'No. I've met her. I've been to her bungalow. You're right, she's obsessively clean.' Rose wondered if it would be breaking any sort of confidence by explaining just who Carol was. From what Geoff had said, it appeared she hadn't told him about Beth. What a traumatic time for the family. Carol would not have been able to confide in her mother or sister. Her problem would have seemed trivial, selfish, even, by comparison with what Sally was going through.

'When? You seem to know absolutely everyone in the county.'

'That's what my father always says.' She decided to take a chance. 'The reason I met her is that Carol is Beth Jones's aunt. Beth's the little girl who's gone missing and I happened to see her abducted.'

'My God, Rose, you never cease to amaze me.' He grinned. 'I wonder what Jack Pearce had to say about that.'

Fortunately, it was not as much as Rose had been expecting, but she kept that to herself.

'No wonder she was so open with me. She couldn't possibly burden her family with her own problems right now.'

Rose nodded. Geoff had confirmed her theory; Carol had been desperate for someone to talk

140

to, even if a stranger had to suffice. 'And if she's thinking of going off with this other man and leaving her children, how on earth is she going to appear in the eyes of her mother and sister?'

'Ah, but that's just the point. She isn't sure if she wants either man. The one she's involved with has become obsessed with her and she says he's starting to put the pressure on. If he's like that now, what's he going to be like if they're together on a permanent basis? And he's threatened to tell her husband. Whether she decides to stay or go her husband's going to hear about it.'

'You're right, it is a mess.' Once more Rose was thankful for her happy marriage. She had never wanted another man whilst David was alive. She felt the heat in her face as she recalled the several short-lived affairs she had had once she had recovered from her grief. Detective Inspector Jack Pearce had outlasted them all by some time. But Geoff Carter, with his reputation, would surely be more capable of understanding Carol's point of view than Rose could.

Geoff shrugged in his laconic manner before saying casually, 'She asked if we could meet again. She claimed she felt better for having talked to me.'

Geoff, twice married and with numerous affairs

behind him, was in his early fifties although, admittedly, he looked younger than his years. With his experience of women he should have more sense than to become involved with someone like Carol. But maybe Geoff was the type of man who would never learn, maybe his ego was too great. Without asking, Rose guessed he would have agreed to her request. 'This man's obsessed with her, you say. If you ask me Carol's a touch obsessional, too.'

'Oh?' He raised an eyebrow. Rose's sharp tone made him wonder if she might be a little jealous.

'You said it yourself. You've been to the place, you clearly remembered the smell of bleach.'

'I don't get you.'

'Don't be thick, Geoff. You said the bungalow was spotless. When I went there it was the same, not a single thing out of place, even the gravel on the drive had been recently raked.'

'But I only saw the kitchen. And it was dark, don't forget. Perhaps unhappy females subjugate their emotions with housework.'

Rose smiled at the idea. 'Very philosophical. Some might, but I certainly wouldn't dream of doing so.'

Geoff grinned at her, 'I've noticed. Not that I'd call you a slut; you're the sort that blitzes the place once a week but it's still bugger the cobwebs.'

'Charming. I'm nowhere near that bad. But who was it who said something along the lines that life's too short to stuff a mushroom?'

'Germaine Greer, or one of her ilk. But there's nothing wrong with your cooking, Rosie.'

She bit back a retort and, instead, said quietly, 'Please don't call me that, Geoff. My name's Rose.' Rosie had been David's name for her. The only other person allowed to use it was Barry Rowe who had introduced her to David and who had picked up the habit from him. 'I must go. Thanks for the cheque.' She picked up her bag from the floor and stood. 'Things to do. At least it's stopped raining.' Through the glass frontage people could be seen passing with their umbrellas now furled and, although the pavements shone wetly, sunlight was reflected in the shop windows opposite.

With much to think about Rose walked uphill towards the Bristol & West Building Society where she paid in the cheque. The staff there knew most of their customers so they exchanged some smalltalk. Then she crossed over to the greengrocer's with its bright displays of fruit and vegetables set out on stalls on the pavement.

Because of the large selection she always bought more than was on her list. The shop also sold jars of exotic pickles and chutneys and loose, dried fruit. These latter items were added to the vegetables in her bag. She would make the cake tomorrow. Christmas was only about six weeks away. Thankfully, unlike in some towns and cities, no lights or decorations were as yet in evidence and in Newlyn and Mousehole the switching on ceremonies were not held until into December. Surely, she reasoned, if the whole commercial nonsense began too soon, with Father Christmases on every street corner, the magic would soon be lost for many children.

The wind was stiffening and already the pavements were beginning to dry. As she waited by the bus stop for a gap in the traffic wide enough to enable her to cross back over the road, Rose glanced down the steep hill which led to Penzance harbour. How different the view was from earlier. The sea was now a cobalt blue, topped with thousands of small, white-capped waves. Light dazzled from its surface. In the gap between the buildings which lined both sides of the road, she caught sight of the familiar blue hull of the *Gry Maritha* as she made her way to St Mary's bearing the necessities of life for the islanders who lived on the Isles of Scilly. In the winter it carried a few passengers, too, but Rose had never made the trip at that time of year. She had heard it was a very rough crossing in the winter. Naturally she had been over to the Scilly Isles on the Scillonian, but that was now docked for repairs. It always made its last trip of the year at the end of October.

There was a gap in the traffic. As she finally managed to cross the road she saw, in the distance, the rain clouds moving out to sea, drifting over towards the Lizard Point where a rainbow began to form an arc.

Now that her shopping was completed, with the additional purchases of dried fruit, the bags weighed heavier than she had anticipated. The plastic handles cut into her hands as she made her way up Causewayhead, where more fruit and vegetables were displayed on stalls in the street, along with cut flowers and hardware and pottery.

The only vehicles allowed access during shop hours were those delivering goods. There were no pavements and the uneven surface was slightly slippery in the parts which were still damp.

She was grateful when she finally reached the car park and was able to offload her bags into the boot of the car.

Once home, she unpacked the food and made a sandwich. This, and a mug of coffee, she took up to the attic where the almost finished oil stood on an easel beneath the north facing windows. The light was perfect to inspect it properly. Yes, the colours were just right. Without vanity, Rose saw that you could almost feel the texture of the granite cottages in the foreground. She even imagined she could smell the almond aroma of the flowering gorse. 'You'll do,' she told it as she bit into the granary bread which she had filled with cheese and salad. But she swore as a slice of tomato slid down her front and on to the floor. That would not have happened to Carol Harte, she thought. Carol would have been seated at a table with a plate in front of her.

Rose sat on a canvas painting stool. Obsessional. Both Carol and the man she was seeing shared the same trait. So what? she asked herself as various ideas formed in her mind, ideas she would not be sharing with Jack.

Arthur was in his spacious kitchen slowly and methodically preparing the evening meal. Not yet fully adept at catering, he knew the task would take him most of the afternoon. Evelyn, as he had always known, had spoilt him. On the farm they had shared the work; the greater part of the outdoor work being his, although Evelyn had always turned a hand when it was lambing or calving time or if one of the workers didn't turn up. Until they had sold up and moved they had never been fully aware of just how much time they had put into the livestock, just how much of a tie they had been.

Once they had moved to their Cotswold house, Evelyn had continued to do most of the housework and cooking. Arthur now felt ashamed he had not done more to help her. Perhaps if he'd . . . No, it wouldn't do to go down that road. Guilt would not bring her back. And if their GP was to be believed he had told Arthur that his wife must have been suffering symptoms for some time. 'And her daughter takes after her, they're both as stubborn as hell and won't confide in anyone,' he muttered. He often found himself talking aloud or arguing with a presenter on the radio. He was not yet used to living alone.

Once more he consulted the recipe book and wondered how women could chat whilst flitting around their kitchens and making cookery look so easy.

With three bedrooms and a separate lounge and dining room, the house was really far too big for him but Arthur had known that when he moved it would have to be somewhere completely different from the cosy home he had shared with his wife. Here, the large rooms with their high ceilings provided a contrast with their beamed Cotswold place and he had deliberately tried to create a more masculine environment. But it was also an investment. He lived on very little; it was something Rose would be able to sell at a good profit when his time came to join Evelyn.

Evelyn's things had been disposed of before the move, but not even Rose knew that he had kept her favourite nightdress and her hair brush in which a few strands of her hair remained. Sentimental old fool, he told himself, as he tasted the beef and wine casserole; a meal he had been led to believe was simple. But all that chopping and adding things at various times had taken an age. The carrots and shallots had been added, the mushrooms would follow in half an hour, then the whole thing would go in the oven to finish cooking.

He laid the table for four, using the dinner service they had had for years. He folded the paper serviettes but they refused to stay in the wine glasses the way they had done for Evelyn. Shrugging, he placed them on the side plates instead, then weighted them down with the butter knives.

Rose did not know that he had also invited Barry and Jenny. He hoped it would be a pleasant surprise. She hadn't mentioned anything in their recent telephone conversations but he was aware that Beth's disappearance was very much on her mind and that she was probably more involved than she had led him to believe. Hopefully, the evening's entertainment would prove to be a distraction. Arthur had contemplated asking Jack but that would have been taking a risk. If the two of them had argued, neither of them would have been comfortable, and nor would he have been.

He listened to the news. There was no mention of Beth. It was almost as if she had never existed.

'Michael was here?' Carol wondered if her mother could hear her heart thudding. It seemed to pound in her ears and her mouth was dry.

'You must've known he would come.' Alice watched her daughter carefully. 'Only you could have given him the address.'

Carol's face reddened. 'Yes. I saw no reason not to. He is Beth's father and he loves her. It would have been cruel to refuse under the circumstances.'

'Does he ring you often?' Alice ran a hand through her short grey hair. She was on the verge of collapse but she had to be strong for Sally. What was going through Carol's mind? Alice knew that closed expression and prayed that there wouldn't be some sort of scene if Michael arrived while Carol was still there.

Sally appeared fresh from the bathroom. She now wore clean but worn jeans, a shirt and a sweatshirt. Her short, blonde hair had been spiked up with either mousse or gel but she hadn't bothered with makeup. It would only have exacerbated the ravages of grief which showed plainly in her face. 'Hello, Carol. How are you?'

Carol hugged her briefly. 'I'm fine,' she said avoiding her mother's eyes. 'More to the point, how are you?'

Sally laughed, but no humour was intended. 'Me? I really don't know any more. It's just like, well, if Beth's dead, then I might as well be, too.'

'No, Sally, you mustn't think like that. You mustn't ever think like that.' Alice said quickly. She could not contemplate losing her daughter as well as her granddaughter. For the first time in her life Alice confronted the truth. Sally was her favourite child and maybe that's where Carol's problems stemmed from.

The bell rang shrilly. The three women froze although they knew it had to be Michael.

It was Carol who went to let him in. Alice and Sally did not hear their brief exchange in the hallway but Michael seemed vaguely rattled as he greeted them both.

'Let me take your mac,' Alice said. 'You're soaking.'

He had walked from the guesthouse where he had taken a room on an indefinite basis. In November, the proprietors were glad of the trade. They had asked his reasons for staying. 'Family problems, I'd rather not talk about it,' he had told them, apparently satisfying their curiosity. Either that, or they were tactful because they hadn't questioned him further. 'What're the police doing?' He addressed the question to Sally. He wanted to be alone with her, to try to offer what little comfort he could, but he would not risk her reaction in front of an audience.

Sally put her hands to her face and shook her head. She didn't want to say it, but Michael deserved the truth. 'They called off the search this morning.'

'They've what?'

'They rang earlier. Oh, they're still making their enquiries, but they've covered all the ground they can think of.'

'Who's in charge of the case?'

'A man named Pearce. Inspector Pearce. He's based at Camborne.'

'Look, I think I'd better go. You and Michael have things to talk about.' Carol glanced at her watch. She had just over twenty-four hours to decide whether to leave John or to live with the consequences of staying. Marcus had made that extremely clear.

'I'm going to speak to him. May I use the phone?'

'Of course.' Sally pointed to a table in the corner of the room upon which it stood.

Carol frowned. Michael had not bothered to acknowledge the fact that she was leaving.

'Goodbye, Carol,' Alice said, not liking the expression on her face. But she didn't receive an answer.

CHAPTER EIGHT

Rose was in the garden when Laura arrived. She was, as usual, on foot and slightly breathless. She and Trevor, like quite a lot of locals, did not possess a car. Many fishermen were happy to travel a hundred or more miles out to sea, but once back on land few of them left Cornwall. 'You're caked in mud,' she commented with the wry smile of a woman who did not have a garden and who could not understand anyone wishing to mess around in one. 'Still, you always were a grubby thing. If it's not earth it's paint. Why don't you leave that and let me buy you a drink? The sun must be over the yardarm somewhere or other.'

Rose had been pulling up the weeds, which, like a lot of the flowers, continued to flourish until late in the year. The wind had dried the grass but the soil was still damp so the groundsel and dandelion shoots came out easily enough. She had also cut back the fuchsia which grew so abundantly in West Cornwall and still bore flowers, even though her father had told her not to do so until February. There was a 'Mrs Popple' with its vivid scarlet and purple flowers which now stood taller than Rose, and the more subtle 'Beauty of Bath', the palest of pink and white.

Rose got up from her kneeling position and rubbed her back. 'I'm going out to dinner. If I start drinking now I won't be able to stand the pace.'

'Jack's seen you pissed before.' Laura stood, hands on her thin hips, her head on one side, grinning at her friend. She could see by the look on Rose's face that she would be able to talk her into it.

'I'm not going out with Jack. Dad's invited me over to his house for a meal.'

'Well, he's seen you the worse for wear as well. Come on, let's have a bit of fun.'

'Honestly Laura, I do not, as you so vulgarly put it, get pissed, just a bit merry at times.'

Laura, whose laughter was more of a screech, scared off a herring gull who had been perched on the roof of Rose's shed, eyeing her as she dug and waiting for the chance to swoop down for the worms. At some point in their evolution they had learnt to copy the blackbirds and stamp on the grass with alternate feet to bring them to the surface. With their scavenging ways and enjoyment of the junk food dropped in the streets, Rose wondered if they would recognise a herring any more.

'If it's just you and Arthur you can afford to come out now. He's not a big drinker. And I've got a bit of gossip for you.' If that didn't do it, nothing would.

Rose chewed her lip. 'Okay. You win. But I'll have to get cleaned up first.'

Laura waited in the sitting-room. She stood in the window recess watching the activity in the bay. There were always more small boats out on a Saturday; solitary fishermen who had to work in an office all week and yachts with their blue or white sails engaged in whatever it was they did out there. Laura may have been married to a fisherman but her experience of the sea was limited to a couple of trips on the Scillonian, one of which she had never forgotten. It had been a summer day and the sea was calm. But once the land was out of sight the boat – which had no stabilisers because of the lack of depth of the sea near the islands – had hit the spot where five channels of water merged. Trevor had stood at the bar, a drink in his hand, quite unconcerned by the pitching and tossing. Laura had only just made it down the stairs to the toilets before she was sick. How her husband went out in far worse conditions than that was beyond her. She could never decide whether fishermen were brave or foolish but it was the way in which they earned their living and, until recently with all the decommissioning, a way of living which had been passed down through the generations.

Since that day she had not allowed herself to imagine what it must be like to be on a trawler in a fullblown storm. Several times she had been on the one of which Trevor was skipper, but only when it was moored in Newlyn harbour. The galley was impressive. There were holes in the wooden table in which the crew could put their mugs. In fact, everything was designed so that the cook could prepare meals without his equipment falling about or burning himself. It was the sleeping quarters which horrified her. A continuous bench lined the accommodation.

Above it was a sort of tunnel with round holes spaced about six feet apart. The men slid into these holes and slept, covered with a duvet, in coffin like surroundings. It must be terribly claustrophobic.

She turned as she heard Rose come into the room. 'Ah, you're ready. You certainly look a tad cleaner. Let's go.'

They didn't walk right down to Newlyn but stopped at the Red Lion, the nearest pub to where Rose lived. It was one of six which served the local community and, like most of them, remained open all day.

'What'll it be? It's my round as I talked you into coming.'

'A bitter shandy, please.'

'My, my, we are being careful.' Laura ordered and paid for their drinks. They stood at the bar near the fire which roared in the grate although the weather had turned milder. 'Out with the gossip, then.'

'I knew you wouldn't be able to wait. Well, you know the Bradley twins, Bradley, that is until they got married.'

Rose nodded. They were almost the same age as Rose and Laura and were identical. Plump and pretty, they had short ginger curls, blue eyes and freckles which made them appear girlish. Rose had never been able to tell them apart. Both of them had married at the same time and had had their two children each almost in tandem. There had been a quarrel some years previously, although she couldn't recall what it was about. Jean had married well, Janet's husband was nearly always unemployed. Perhaps the issue had been money. It was the only difference in their lives. 'What about them?'

'You won't believe this but I saw Janet the other day and she said Jean's always been jealous of her.'

'Why? They're so very much alike. And, if anything, it should be the other way around.'

'Precisely, which is why it makes it more intriguing. But don't you remember them at school? They were always in fierce competition with one another.' She paused. 'Of course you don't.' Laura had known Rose for so long that she often forgot they had not grown up together. 'Anyway, there's Jean, with her lovely house and plenty of money, in a far better situation than Janet, but Jean has run off with Janet's layabout husband.'

'What?

'There, I knew you wouldn't believe it.'

'But it's not just that, the money side. I was thinking of it from the husbands' point of view' Rose laughed, seeing the peculiarity of the situation. 'They're identical, for goodness sake. Why would Robert choose his wife's twin to have an affair with?'

'If he did make the choice. If Jean was jealous, she may have made a play for him.'

'Or he might have thought he'd get a part of her share of any divorce settlement.'

'How cynical, Rose, my sweet. But you might be right.' Laura swallowed the last of her vodka and tonic. 'Another one?'

'One more. But only the one. I'll buy.' Rose got out her purse. What Laura had described was a strange situation but she had seen what jealousy could do to families, even when there was no reason for it. When a member of your own family turned on you it could be far worse than if it was someone you barely knew.

The barmaid served their drinks then retreated to the corner where she was in deep conversation with some other customers. There was the click of pool balls from the table where two men were playing. Rose watched them for a moment but her mind was really elsewhere.

'Why are you smiling?'

'The thing is, Laura, I can't tell them apart. How will I know which one to commiserate with if I happen to see one of them in the street?'

'Good point.' Laura had the same problem. It was easier when they were together, there were minute differences in their appearance, but apart, it was virtually impossible to guarantee getting the name right. 'Best not to say anything then.'

As gossip went, it was not as juicy as it could have been but it still intrigued Rose.

Laura sensed that Rose was ready to go home so she did not try to persuade her to stay. 'Have a nice evening,' she said as Rose pulled on her jacket and made for the door. 'And give Arthur my love.'

'I will. See you soon.'

Rose walked home slowly. It was a perfect winter's afternoon. The sun shone, although without any real warmth. Already it was lower in the sky than it had been a week or so ago. The coastline was visible for the whole of its sweeping length. The water in the harbour had turned a milky blue and a trawler chose that moment to turn in through the gaps, seagulls following in its wake. For several minutes she stood and wondered how it would be possible to capture that exact shade of translucent blue on canvas.

Come on, she told herself, there's the ironing to do before you start getting ready to go out, real work will have to wait.

The tiresome chore was done whilst she listened to Radio 4. When she'd put the ironing board back in its place in the larder she changed stations to listen to the local news on Radio Cornwall. There was no mention of Bethany Jones. Perhaps the local press had covered the story but she hadn't bought a paper for several days. It was four days since she had seen Beth. So very much could have happened to a little girl during that time. Rose felt sick. Why didn't I realise something was wrong, she thought. Why didn't Beth make a fuss? But the answer was obvious, the man was someone whom she knew. In which case, why hadn't Jack found him yet? Surely the family would have provided the names and addresses of everyone they had ever had any contact with, no matter how minimal it might have been.

And had Jack managed to find a way to speak to Susan's daughter, Kate? All these things were going around in her mind as she showered, scrubbing at her nails to remove the stains left by the earth from her gardening.

She put on a taupe skirt with a matching

jacket and a silk vest of a slightly lighter shade. Her hair she left loose. Once her makeup was on she painted her nails a pale ginger colour and sat in the sitting-room, admiring the view until they were dry. Since the last time she had looked out of the window, a salvage tug had anchored in the bay. They sometimes stayed for weeks, just sitting there until a job came along or they had to go to Falmouth to refuel. It must be a very boring, if well paid, job, she decided. It was now dark and the tug was fully lit and made a lovely picture. I could try that, Rose thought. Why not? It would be an entirely new view of the bay with the Mount only there as a dark backdrop. Her fingers itched to pick up a pencil and start sketching but there wasn't time. It would have to wait.

The taxi arrived on time and she was driven to her father's house. He must have been watching for her because he opened the door before she had had a chance to knock. 'You look lovely. Come on in and have a drink.'

Rose looked up at him questioningly. She could hear voices.

'Barry and Jenny. I invited them, too. I hope you don't mind.'

'Not at all. You know how much I like them.'

They were seated in the large lounge where

a fire burned in the grate and small lamps lit the scene. Despite her father's attempts at masculinity he had still managed to produce a room that was welcoming in the evenings.

Arthur poured his daughter a drink and handed it to her. 'We'll eat in about half an hour if that's all right with everyone. I just hope it'll be all right.'

'Of course it will,' Jenny told him with a smile.

Rose watched the woman with whom Barry had become involved, although she wasn't quite sure to what extent. It was not a question she could, or would ask him. She was almost the same height as him, with a rounded body that was not quite plump. Her fair hair was curly. Parted on one side it hung to just below her shoulders. She was not classically beautiful, not really even pretty, but her smile made her face come alive. It was a smile that no one could fail to respond to. She, too, had dressed with care in deference to the age of their host who, they imagined, expected such things.

As for Arthur; Rose had always thought he looked a great deal like the Duke of Edinburgh, not that he thought so himself. He laughed whenever she mentioned the fact.

'Have you heard any more about Beth?' Barry

asked, knowing it would be pointless to avoid the subject. He failed to notice Arthur frowning at his question.

'No, and the press seem to have stopped reporting anything.'

'That poor mother. She must be going through hell,' Jenny added, unable to imagine her own feelings if anything happened to Polly. Nichola had vowed she would never marry so Polly might be the only grandchild she ever had.

'I don't understand it. If what you saw is any indication, Rose, then the child knew the person who took her. Surely they ought to be able to find him.'

'I was thinking exactly the same earlier, Dad. But Jack knows what he's doing.'

Arthur sighed. 'I suppose so. I'm just worried you'll take matters into your own hands again. You're such a worry at times, Rose Trevelyan.'

Rose smiled. 'You're beginning to sound like Jack. I don't want two men like that in my life. Shall I pour us some more drinks?'

'Yes. Please do. I'll see to the rest of the meal.' Arthur left the room knowing that Rose had wanted the subject to be changed. But why? Was she making plans that she had no wish for him to be privy to? It wouldn't surprise him in the least, although what she could do that the police couldn't was beyond him.

'Mm,' he said with satisfaction as he entered the kitchen and smelt the richness of the casserole as it reheated in the oven. The potatoes were roasting nicely and the vegetables wouldn't take more than a few minutes. He wondered if he ought to have made a starter but decided that might have been too ambitious for his first attempt at entertaining people other than his daughter. Besides, there was plenty of fruit and cheese and enough casserole for two helpings each if they wanted it.

'That was excellent,' Barry commented when they had eaten, although he didn't quite manage to disguise his surprise. 'You'll have to give me some tips.'

'Thank you.' Arthur reddened slightly. He was thrilled it had all gone so well.

'Did I mention that Jenny and I are going on holiday?'

'No.' Rose and Arthur answered in unison, their surprise equally as apparent. Barry had never taken a holiday in all the years they had known him.

'We're going in January. Two weeks somewhere in the sun. The shop'll be quiet then and Daphne has assured me she'll be able to cope. It means her working an extra day each week, but she said she'll be glad of the money.'

Over the years Barry had had an assortment of part-time staff, but some months previously he had taken on Daphne Hill on a full time basis. The idea had been to give him more leisure time as he also had the print works in Camborne to run. It had taken Rose ages to persuade him to actually use that spare time for leisure. Now he was taking it a step further, which was a good sign; perhaps, of course, Jenny was responsible for his new attitude.

The evening came to an end when they saw that Arthur was beginning to look tired. Barry and Jenny had walked and were returning home the same way, Rose rang for a taxi. Stone's, the local firm, were cheap and reliable and all the drivers knew her and chatted about her work when they drove her anywhere.

'Please be careful, darling,' Arthur said as they waited for the cab to arrive.

Rose knew he was not referring to her short trip home. 'I will, Dad,' she replied, kissing him on the cheek by way of reassurance. Perhaps she ought to keep out of things, her father had enough to worry about. But with the ideas which had been racing around her mind all evening, she thought it was probably impossible she'd be able to simply do nothing.

It took her a long time to get to sleep that night because she had had an idea but absolutely no way of knowing how to implement it.

On Saturday morning Doreen Clarke was dressed for the weather. Her raincoat was tightly belted and her headscarf was knotted firmly in place. Over her arm was the wicker basket she always used for her shopping. She hated plastic carrier bags and the way in which they dug into her hands. She usually drove in to Penzance at the weekend but she'd decided against it as Cyril's brother was coming later that day. She would shop in Hayle instead.

On the opposite side of the road she saw Susan and Katy. Katy was holding her mother's hand. For once the child looked relaxed as she pointed to something amongst the reeds. Doreen waved but they didn't see her. I wonder if Rose has said anything to Jack, she thought as she made her way towards the baker's where she now bought her bread. Once, she had made it herself, but that was in the days when Cyril was in full-time employment and she didn't have to go out to work. Fortunately his redundancy hadn't come until after her boys had left home.

At least Katy's with her parents, not like that poor little Beth, Doreen told herself as she waited to cross the road. She decided she would telephone Rose later to see if there had been any developments on either count.

Jack spent Saturday afternoon at home. He had done all he could at the station and was satisfied that a tactful, fatherly officer would be despatched to the local schools on Monday morning. He had had to have his decision endorsed from above but when he explained that there might be a connection between the two, possibly three children the hesitation had only been brief. Anything was worth a try at this stage.

He had rung Rose's number. There was no reply but he decided not to leave a message. Sitting in his armchair he wondered if the rain would ever stop. With a beer in his hand he watched some sport but it wasn't long before he realised he was bored. He picked up the telephone and got someone at Camborne to check the computer to see if the name Overton appeared for any reason. 'Call me back at home, please,' he said. 'I'll be here for an hour or so.'

And then what? He really ought to go and visit his mother. It was over a fortnight since he had seen her. She was a proud and independent woman and wouldn't dream of asking him to come and he knew he should make more of an effort. When he did visit he never stayed long. As much as she loved her son, Amelia Pearce only endured short visits. But she always takes an interest in my job, Jack thought. Perhaps he could see if she had any suggestions.

Twenty minutes later the telephone rang. 'There's nothing on anyone named Overton, sir,' he was told.

Jack put on a jacket and picked up his car keys and drove to Newlyn then up to the village of Paul where his mother lived in a cottage which was badly in need of decoration – although she refused to have anyone in to do it, even though Jack had offered to pay the bill. 'I like it as it is,' she'd told him. 'And it's not as if it's dirty. At my age people don't want change. You'll find that out for yourself one day, young man.' Jack had smiled at that. He was fifty; to his mother, now seventy-seven, he probably did seem young.

Amelia was frowning when she answered the door. 'Oh, it's you.' Her expression changed. She was always pleased to see Jack. 'You haven't brought your lady friend to see me for some time. Is everything all right between you?' she asked as he followed her to the kitchen. His mother drank more tea than anyone he had ever met.

'Yes. Everything's fine. She's been busy lately so I haven't seen much of her myself.'

'Still doing your job for you, is she?'

Jack grinned. His mother didn't miss much. 'Hopefully, this time, she's not.'

'The missing child?'

'Yes.'

'Ah.' Amelia turned her attention to the tea things.

Jack noticed that although she was smartly dressed and her hair pinned up neatly, there was more of a stoop in her shoulders than he recalled being there before. 'Ah, what?'

'She won't be found alive, will she?'

'That's what we're beginning to think.'

'I spoke to Norma Penhalligon about it only this morning. She told me the child's father turned up last night.'

Norma Penhalligon? That was a name Rose had come out with, too. Mrs Penhalligon was Sally's landlady. He knew what Rose was like when it came to knowing people, but he hadn't expected the same of his mother. 'You know her?'

'We went to school together. You must've heard me mention her name.'

Jack couldn't recall her doing so, probably because until the case had started he had never met the woman. He had not met many of his mother's friends for some time now because she discouraged them from visiting her. He did know, however, that her telephone bill was higher than most because this was the way in which she preferred to keep in touch with the outside world. 'What's Norma like?'

'What an odd question,' she said as she handed him his tea. 'A normal old lady, like me.'

Jack smiled to himself. He did not see his mother as normal. 'I mean, is she trustworthy?' He was thinking about the visit to Carol Harte's house she had made with Rose and if there was more to it than concern for the sister.

Why would the pair of them have put themselves out? In Rose's case it was probably due to her innate curiosity but Norma Penhalligon may have had ulterior motives.

'As much as anyone can be. She would never do anyone any harm and she's not one to gossip, and that, as you know, is damn unusual round here. You can't possibly think she's got anything to do with it.'

Not until this minute, Jack thought. The woman obviously hadn't taken the child herself but she knew the family and might have a reason for wishing Beth or her mother harm. 'No, of course not,' he answered. His mother was discreet but he could not risk her ringing her old friend and hinting that she might be a suspect.

'You don't know where you're going with this,' Amelia stated, seeing in her only child's face what was going through his mind.

'No, we really don't. Rose claims the child went willingly. It has to be someone that knows them.'

'Rose?' Amelia smiled. 'I might have guessed. I suppose you're not best pleased that she's involved, however peripherally'

'You're dead right I'm not.'

'Is that the time? My favourite radio programme's on in a minute.' Amelia stood and walked over to the worktop where her old but reliable radio was placed.

Hint taken, Jack thought as he, too, stood. He kissed his mother's wrinkled, powdery cheek. 'I'll be off then.'

'Jack, dear, look to her relatives. If you ask me, someone's not talking, or, at least not telling the whole truth.'

He nodded and let himself out, as his mother was busy fiddling with the volume control.

It had stopped raining. He started to make his way home, driving past the church in the village of Paul where the last woman to speak Cornish as her natural language was buried. The roads were wet and droplets of rain sparkled in the hedgerows but a drying wind was picking up. Jack no longer cared whether or not it was wet; his frustration was building up and he was beginning to feel useless. The empty evening stretched ahead of him with no Rose to share it. She had told him she was having dinner with her father. He wished that he had also been invited. Maybe Barry Rowe fancied a drink or something to eat. He was far more sociable in recent months.

But when he got home and dialled Barry's number there was no reply. The man hadn't even got an answering machine for the flat although there was one for the shop line. Quite who he expected to ring the shop after closing time was beyond Jack, but he supposed Barry had his own reasons for this.

After a makeshift meal he washed up then read for a while. At ten thirty feeling exhausted even though he had done nothing, he went to bed and tossed restlessly until sleep finally overtook him. But not for long.

He woke at three and went to the kitchen to make tea. The cushioned floor covering was cold beneath his bare feet. The flat had become chilly since the heating had switched itself off.

A dream had woken him; one of those endless, meaningless dreams in which numerous people appear who bear no resemblance to anyone in real life. Jack could not understand why such a harmless dream had woken him for it had no nightmare quality, only that it had left him feeling exhausted.

Shivering, he took the tea back to bed. It was still warm from the heat of his body beneath the duvet. He wished that Rose was beside him. It seemed an age since he had spent some proper time with her. She would have woken when he did, she always sensed his first movements almost before he made them. Was she sleeping now, he wondered. Her nights were occasionally disturbed, and Beth would be very much on her mind. Odd that she hadn't mentioned her, or shown signs of becoming more involved with the family. More likely, she had done so and was keeping the fact from him.

He began to think back over the day. The sense of frustration returned. The schools thing was all set up but he had not been able to contact Michael

Poole who had rung the station that morning whilst Jack was engaged on a long telephone conversation concerning another case. Twice the man had tried to get through but he had not left a number. Jack, assuming he was at his Looe address, had tried to get hold of him there. Only when he had left the station and called in to see his mother did he learn that Poole, contrary to what he had been advised, was in the area. Consequently, he had not previously thought of ringing Sally's number. He did so after leaving his mother's house. By then he was too late.

'Yes, he was here earlier but he's gone now,' Alice Jones had told him. 'He drove down last night. He couldn't not come, he said, and I don't blame him.'

Jack understood that. No matter that their presence would make no difference, people always wanted to be on the spot. 'Do you know where I can reach him?' he had asked.

'No. We only know that he's found some accommodation in Marazion.'

'Does he have a mobile phone?'

'If he does, we don't have the number and he asked to use this phone earlier. Oh,' Alice stopped speaking. It sounded as though she had placed her hand over the mouthpiece and was talking to someone else. 'Sorry. That was Sally. I made her lie down for a while but she heard the phone.'

175

Jack knew the effect it would have had on her. Initially, each time it rang she would have been expecting good news. By now her expectations would have swung the other way. 'Have you any idea why he wanted to speak to me, Mrs Jones?'

'All I know was that he was upset about the search being called off, but if there was anything else, he didn't say.' She paused. 'I'm glad he's here, he's a good man, Inspector Pearce, and he's never missed making payments for little Beth.'

So he was making payments for the child. He must look into that aspect further. 'The search hasn't been called off altogether. We've still got plenty of officers out looking for Beth.' But not as many as there were, and not as many as I would like, he had thought. 'If Mr Poole should contact you again would you ask him to give me a ring at Camborne or on this number.' He recited his mobile number, the one supplied with the job. The private numbers of police officers were always unlisted for safety reasons.

Alice had promised to pass on the message but no call had come. It wouldn't now, not at three thirty in the morning.

Jack turned off the light and managed to fall asleep again some time later.

* * *

Carol knew the real reason for her distress and she hated herself for it; that and her cowardice. It was all based on guilt of course. What a weight of it she had had to bear and it would never end now. How pointless her actions had become, and how very, very selfish. But she had always been selfish. What was amazing was that the whole plan had been accepted, although not by everyone because there were people who had been left in the dark.

Even though she was used to being alone a lot of the time, the bungalow had an empty, lifeless feel to it that evening. As it grew dark she put on all the lights and pulled the curtains. How strange it had been to see Michael again after such a long time. Now and then they spoke over the telephone but never for long. Carol was too afraid that the truth might come out.

She paced the immaculate lounge, listening to the wind rattling the bare branches of the trees and the faint creak of the shed door which told her that the wind was westerly; a kind wind, usually a mild one which often brought rain. If only someone would be kind to me, she thought, ashamed of the self-pity when she had brought it all on herself.

She walked to the window and drew aside one of the curtains. Leaning her hot head against the cool glass she saw nothing but the blackness outside. 'Beth, oh, Beth, what I did was so very wrong,' she whispered.

No one would ever forgive her for what she had done to the child. And how much of the truth Marcus had guessed at she couldn't bear to think about.

Marcus realised that the days he had taken off to be with Carol had been wasted. Her husband and children were away, as arranged, yet he had hardly seen her.

He had not really meant what he had said about telling her husband. He loved her but he didn't want her on those terms, and if she had decided that she didn't want him, then he would have been hurting the man unnecessarily. What he really wanted was a straight answer and he'd hoped to shock her into making one.

Carol had refused to see him again until Sunday. 'I'll call in on the way to collect the children,' she had promised.

Naturally, Marcus had to assume her answer would be no. If she needed time to think about it there was no point in continuing.

Of course, part of the reason for her state of mind was the disappearance of her niece. She loved the little girl. But he also gathered, from unguarded comments, that the same feelings were not extended to her sister, Sally.

With no other plans for a Saturday night, Marcus took himself to the cinema. Anything was better than sitting at home alone and he did not feel like socialising. The Savoy, in Causewayhead, now had three screens and a plaque which proudly announced the fact that films had been shown continuously ever since it had opened, despite the war. It was the only cinema to have done so. Marcus was aware of this but as he sat through a film, the plot of which only vaguely registered, he couldn't have cared less.

Was it a coincidence that Carol's family were all away at the time Beth was taken from that beach? But why would she wish to harm a child she claimed to love so much, he asked himself as the credits finally rolled and people were getting up, ready to leave.

He put on his coat and followed them out into the night. He had watched an early performance, it was only just after eight. If he hadn't met Carol he would have been anticipating a night out with friends, not about to return home alone. I'll ring her, he decided as, hands in his pockets against the chill, he headed towards his flat which was situated up a side street just past the railway station.

A train was pulling out, a 125, brightly lit, the passengers clearly visible. Marcus wished he were on it, wherever it was going. But I'd not get an answer from Carol then, he realised. Deep down he knew that solution would probably be for the best, but the idea of it happening was unbearable.

Walking past a plate glass window of an unlit shop, Marcus realised that the hunch shouldered man reflected there was himself. If it hadn't been for his height and his close cropped blond hair he would have thought it was a stranger.

Back at his modern, purpose built flat he felt glad of the warmth and familiar surroundings. He had never married because he had never found anyone he wanted to share his life with, not until he met Carol. He would have taken on her children, too, if that was what she wanted. But he had no idea what she did want.

He picked up his cordless phone and carried it out to the kitchen where he pulled down the blind because the people in the building opposite could see straight in when the light was on. There was some beer in the fridge. He might as well have one. In his anxiety he poured it too fast and it frothed up over the edge of the glass and left a pool on the worktop surface. Disregarding this, he took a sip, wiped the foam from his mouth and dialled Carol's number. It rang for a long time. There was no reply, nor did the answering machine click on. She had told him that she was staying in, that she needed time alone to think.

So where, exactly, is she? he wondered as he made another call, this time to order an Indian takeaway. He was told it would be ready in forty minutes. Going to collect it would give him something to do, for which he was grateful.

Admitting that showed the state of his own mind. Never before had he felt so restless and so in need of Carol's company.

CHAPTER NINE

Michael Poole was unable to face the meal placed in front of him. There was nothing wrong with the food: it was a perfectly cooked Cornish breakfast with a generous helping of the local Hog's Pudding. He had no appetite since the police had first visited him and everything he ate tasted the same. However, he knew that he must eat something if he were not to become ill. He had sat drinking cups of the strong tea until his eggs had gone cold, feeling it wrong to be sitting in front of a full plate whilst his daughter might be starving, or worse. If she was even alive, he amended grimly.

'I'm sorry, I really can't finish this,' he said when the landlady came to clear the table.

'I understand, dear. No one feels like eating when they've got problems. Can I get you some toast?'

'No, I'm fine, thanks.' He went back up to his room and tried the number for the Camborne police station again. This time he was in luck; Inspector Pearce was available.

'Thank you for getting back to me. What can I do for you, Mr Poole?' Jack asked. Several cups of black coffee had not repaired the damages of a disturbed night but his mood improved because there might be a lead here.

'I want to know why you've called off the search. You can't just give up like that.'

Jack explained, as patiently as he was able, that this was not strictly the case. 'What it actually means is that some of the men have been stood down. We still have a large number of people out there looking for Beth.'

'I see. I just thought . . . well, Sally said.' He stopped, unable to form a complete sentence because the reality of the situation hit him. The police believed, as he had come to do, that Beth would not be found alive.

'Mr Poole, may I ask you what made you decide to come down here?'

'Goddamit, man, what do you think? You

asked me to stay put, but would you have done?'

No, Jack thought, I wouldn't. 'I'd very much like to speak to you in person. Would sometime today be convenient?' The man's anger had sounded genuine, the outburst of an innocent person, but over the telephone it could have been faked and they could not afford to take anything for granted. It was an unpalatable fact, but parents did harm their children then give tearful media interviews begging for their safe return when they knew that would never be possible. Although what Poole's motive could be was not clear. Beth didn't live with him, in fact, he hadn't seen her since she was a toddler so it wasn't a case of her continual whining or crying getting on his nerves. But there had been the custody application; it might be a case of if he couldn't have her neither could Sally. But the case had not made it to the courts. Everyone had agreed that Sally was a fit mother and that Poole would have had great difficulty in bringing up the child himself. And that had been almost two years ago, why would he wait until now to act? Jack sighed. Perhaps the answer was obvious; immediate action would have drawn attention to himself.

'Inspector Pearce, I can meet you sometime this afternoon if that's convenient. Only I promised I'd go and see Sally this morning.'

This afternoon it was then. He did not want to be accused of making things hard for the father of a missing child. 'What time would suit you?'

'Two o'clock?'

'That's fine. Where can I find you?'

Michael had expected to be asked to come to the station for some sort of formal interview. He did not want to take the Inspector to his hotel bedroom, it did not seem fitting for the occasion and they might be overheard in the guests' lounge. 'How about the Godolphin Arms?'

That was fine by Jack, although he'd have to stick to coffee. If Poole had a couple of drinks under his belt he might be more inclined to let something slip. It would be interesting to meet him, to sum up the father of Sally's child in person.

He walked over to the window and stared out, hardly noticing the few passing cars, their occupants no doubt on their way to relatives for Sunday lunch or to visit one of the supermarkets. Even in Cornwall Sunday was beginning to lose its different feel from the rest of the week. It had once been a day off for everyone, apart from pub landlords, hoteliers and the women who had stayed in the kitchen to cook the traditional roast. Now the big stores remained open as did many of the smaller shops once the season had started.

Knowing that there was little more he could do until his arranged meeting with Poole, Jack decided to ring Rose. There was no reply. 'Give me a call when you've got the time,' he said after her voice had told him to leave a message. He had not meant to sound abrupt but life seemed to be frustrating him in all directions.

As she woke on Sunday morning Rose heard the familiar whine of the wind in the chimneybreast of the blocked off fireplace in her bedroom. At least it wasn't raining. She tried to keep Sundays as a rest day but in the winter, if the weather allowed, she would work out of doors because there was so little opportunity to do so with the shortened days.

Still in her dressing gown, she made coffee and watched the waves rolling in and breaking against the concave Promenade wall. It was a magnificent sight. Spray was sent high in the air, threaded with rainbow colours as the sun backlit it. Further out the bright red salvage tug swung on its anchor. The sky might be clear and blue but she could see by the way the flags on the Queen's Hotel were blowing that the wind was from the east. It would be too cold to work outside for long. However, the whole day lay in front of her and she had no idea what to do with it. She smiled at her indecision. It was typical. How often had she wished for such a day when she could lie in the bath, have a face pack, maybe, then laze around reading. This was what she always wished for but she had too much energy, too much zest for life to do so.

Jack would still be fully occupied, her friends had all made arrangements and even her father had told her he was driving over to Redruth to meet a man with whom he had become acquainted on one of his previous visits to Cornwall. As she wandered back to the kitchen Sally Jones's face came into her mind. Surely no one could look more grief-stricken. I must speak to her again, I must see if there's anything I can do no matter how trivial or useless it might seem.

Just over an hour later she was on her way to Marazion. It was still relatively early for a Sunday morning but she doubted Sally would still be in bed, if she had slept at all.

Traffic was light and the supermarkets didn't open until ten so she made good time.

Having parked she walked through the quiet Sunday streets. Curtains were still drawn at some of the windows of the small terraced cottages. The high tide was beginning to recede but it would be some time before the causeway leading to St Michael's Mount was walkable. The occasional car or van used it, too, at low tide. Rose had often wondered what it must be like to live there. Unlike an island where you knew you were totally cut off, twice in every twenty-four hours access by foot was possible, otherwise you could only reach the mainland by way of one of the small boats that ferried people backwards and forwards. But if you wanted a late night out and there was a full tide, how did you get back home? Rose realised that you probably didn't, that you made arrangements to stay with someone.

She was about to ring the bell with the name Jones above it when the front door of the house opened. Norma Penhalligon was as surprised as Rose when they came face to face so suddenly. 'I was just going out. You startled me, dear, but it's nice to see you again. Have you come to see Sally?'

'Yes. How is she? I mean, do you think she's up to receiving visitors?'

'It would seem so, there's two with her now, as well as her mum.'

'Two?'

'The sister, and the ex-boyfriend.'

Rose had guessed he would not have been able to stay away for long no matter what his relationship with Sally was now like. 'Perhaps I'd better leave it then.' But before she could decide either way they both looked up as they heard raised voices from the floor above.

'You've always wanted what was mine. Always. Sometimes I think you must actually hate me.'

Norma looked at Rose and raised her eyebrows. It was hard to tell whose voice it was. 'I don't think a visit's a good idea after all. Still, it's hardly surprising, the tension must be getting to them all.' Norma sighed and picked at a thread hanging from a buttonhole on her coat. 'It seems far longer than five days since I saw Beth leaving here with her mother. She looked so cute, too, in her new jacket. You know, one of those brightly coloured padded ones all the little ones wear these days. They're warm, but practical. You can put them in the washing machine, not like when my ones were small. Winter coats had to be dry-cleaned in them days.' She stopped as footsteps sounded on the landing and a man made his way down the stairs. 'Hello, it's Mrs Penhalligon, isn't it?'

She nodded. They had met briefly yesterday. 'And this is Rose Trevelyan. Rose, this is Michael Poole, Beth's father.' They shook hands. 'It was Rose who saw the man who took Beth.'

'You did? The police told me they had a witness. I never expected to meet her. I didn't know you actually knew Sally.'

'I didn't. I didn't meet her until after it happened. I just called in to see if there was anything I could do.' Rose studied the good-looking man. He had short, fair hair and was smartly, but casually dressed. But the lines in his face and his drawn expression showed how he felt.

'I think it would be better not to disturb her right now. She and Carol have had a row and they're both upset. Perhaps you could come back some other time.' He looked down at the black and white tiles of the entrance hall which Norma kept spotlessly clean. 'If Sally hadn't left me this wouldn't have happened. I'm not blaming her for it, far from it. It's my fault, I should have been more persuasive, talked her into staying, and if that failed I should at least have insisted upon proper access. But she really convinced me it was better the way she wanted it. What a fool I was.'

Norma and Rose had no idea what to say to

the man. Nothing would make any difference now. In any case there would be tremendous guilt on all sides. And blame. And that could tear families apart.

'I'm going back to the guesthouse. They know where I am if they need me. And I'm meeting Inspector Pearce later on. I want to know exactly what they're doing.'

Poor Jack. Rose knew she would see little of him until the case was over, but she felt guilty for not having telephoned just to see how he was. 'Goodbye,' she said. It was hardly appropriate to add something along the lines of it being nice meeting him.

More footsteps were heard as Michael shut the door behind him. These were lighter, those of a woman. Carol Harte came slowly down the stairs, her hand resting on the polished wood of the banister. She looked older and more defeated than when Rose had last seen her. 'Oh.' She jumped. She had not realised that she was not alone.

'Are you all right, maid?' Norma asked.

She shook her head. 'Not really. No, I'm not at all all right.' Tears filled her eyes. She wiped them away impatiently with her fingertips. 'I just feel so bloody alone at the moment.'

Geoff Carter had sensed this but Rose wondered if it was an act. After all, she had a husband and children, a sister and mother and a lover.

'Do you want to come in for a coffee?'

'It's very kind of you, Norma, but I need to get away from here for a while.' She only hesitated for a second before adding, 'Why don't you come out to my place for one? I could do with some sane company. Why don't you both come? I can drop you back, Norma.'

Rose could not resist this invitation. This was a chance to get to know Carol better, a chance, maybe, to put her theory to the test. She accepted the offer.

Laura had mentioned the Bradley twins and their jealousies, which she had found odd. Rose had imagined that all twins were especially close, almost telepathic at times, but it was possible that as they had grown older they had needed to find their own identity and the bond had been broken. Thinking about them had led her to question the relationship between Carol and Sally, even more so since she had overheard part of their quarrel. She hoped Carol would tell them what it was about.

Norma went in Carol's car. This caused Rose

some frustration. Carol may confide in the older woman before they reached their destination. But the journey was not long enough for much of a conversation to have taken place.

She pulled up behind Carol's car on the neatly raked gravel. The bungalow was built on high ground and the wind tugged at their hair and clothing. For once Rose was wearing a skirt. The tan corduroy swung to one side revealing the tops of her boots. The last of the autumn leaves were sent scurrying across the lawn. Carol's flowerbeds were empty; the soil dug and turned over. No doubt there would be daffodil bulbs beneath its surface and bedding plants to follow later, but Rose preferred some greenery and coloured heathers all the year round.

'It's so damn cold,' Carol said as she unlocked the front door. It was not that cold now that wind had veered to the south, but Carol was in a state of shock, it was emotional distress taking its toll.

They were shown into the lounge with its view over the rolling countryside. It was so very green after all the rain, so very English.

'Tea or coffee?' she asked as she gestured for her guests to sit down. She stood in the doorway, her dark hair framing a face as white as the carpet beneath their feet. The dark smudges beneath her eyes made her look ill. She seemed to be almost at breaking point.

'Let me do it,' Norma said as she took off her coat in a businesslike manner. 'You look worn out. Sit down, dear. I'm sure I'll be able to find everything.'

Carol nodded and sank into an armchair. Rose had chosen the settee. 'Are you feeling any better?' she asked to break the silence, but not expecting the answer she received.

'No. Worse, if anything. I had a row with Sally. I mean, now, of all times. I don't know how I let it happen. I should have held my tongue. And so should she. Even now, with Beth missing, she can't let go.'

'Let go of what?' Rose spoke softly. She was on the verge of learning something and she didn't want to scare Carol off the subject.

She sighed. 'It's been the same all our lives. I know she's a bit younger than me and probably resented my being born first – that happens in lots of families – but anything I've ever had or wanted, she's either taken, or tried to take away from me. What makes it worse is that is exactly what she accused me of doing this morning.'

So it had been Sally's voice they had heard. However, Carol's self-pity seemed a little excessive considering what her sister had actually lost. And then Carol spoke again. Rose leant forward, her hands resting on the pile of her skirt. Her hair hid one side of her face from Carol.

'The trouble is I've never really tried to stop her. When I was small it seemed natural for her to have the things I wanted. It became a habit. Oh, Rose, I've made some terrible mistakes, but one of them was worse than anyone else could possibly have made.'

There was no doubt that Carol was obsessive; the clean white carpet covering the floor of a house where two small children lived was further proof of that. But now, looking at her eyes which sparkled too brightly and the face with its two vivid spots of colour, Rose thought she might also be neurotic, possibly even mentally ill; the sort of woman who thought the world was against her. Yes, everyone suffered a touch of paranoia once in a while, but surely not to this extent. Unless, of course, it was simply a case of exaggerated sibling rivalry. It was not a nice thought but there was always the chance that Carol was resenting the amount of attention her sister was receiving at the moment.

'I'm sorry. I hardly know you, I shouldn't be burdening you like this. I suppose it's because I feel you're part of it, having been there on Tuesday.

And whatever you may think, believe me, I do know exactly what Sally's going through. That's probably the reason why she snapped.'

'Sometimes it's easier to say things to a stranger.' Rose wanted to bring up the subject of the boyfriend but could not do so without giving away the fact that Geoff had told her. Carol would know she had been betrayed.

Norma appeared with a tray. She set it on a small table. She had found pots and made tea and coffee, taking her time because she realised that Rose was the sort of woman Carol might confide in. As for herself, well, she was probably considered as being too old to understand her problem even though she had seen far more of life than Carol. And Norma had a good idea what her problem might be. 'Who's for what?' She poured two coffees and tea for herself. 'Put some sugar in it, Carol. It'll do you good. Now, what was all that about earlier? I couldn't help but overhear the shouting.'

Rose bit her lip. Now was not the time to smile, either Norma didn't waste words, or tact was not her strong point.

'You must have heard, too,' Carol said with a frown as she asked herself what Rose had been doing in the downstairs hallway.

'Not really. I'd only just arrived when you

came down the stairs. I bumped into Norma as she was on her way out.'

'God, I've caused everyone so much trouble. I'm sorry, Norma, I didn't realise you were busy.'

''Tisn't important. I can go up to the churchyard this afternoon. I tidy my parents' graves every month or so,' she added, by way of explanation to Rose. 'Sunday seems to be the appropriate day to do it somehow.'

They both turned to Carol who had started to cry quietly. 'I miss that little girl,' she said through her tears. 'No one knows how much I love her. I should never have done what I did. Never.' The tears flowed harder. Rose got a tissue from the cellophane packet she kept in her handbag and walked over to where Carol was sitting. 'Here, use this,' she said. Then, more gently, 'What was it you did, Carol?'

Carol blew her nose and shook her head. 'Oh, nothing really. I'm so bloody distraught I don't know what I'm saying. That row, that's what's done it, it's really unnerved me.'

'When are your two kiddies coming home?' Norma thought Carol required someone or something else to occupy her thoughts rather than her own self-pity. It had been a bad idea, sending them to stay with their grandparents.

'Tonight. I'm picking them up around teatime.'

'Good. I'm sure they'll have missed you. I think we'll leave you in peace now. I'm sure Rose won't mind dropping me back. It's not out of your way, is it, dear?'

'Not at all. I'm going that way. I'm going back to Newlyn.'

They were about to get into the car when a third vehicle turned in at the gate. Carol, seeing them off from the door, had one hand to her mouth, the other steadying herself against the lintel.

The man who got out of the car might have been Carol's husband but Rose guessed, judging by her reaction, that it was more likely to be the boyfriend. Bugger it, she thought. If we'd stayed just a few more minutes things might have become really interesting. She gave a wave then got into the car and turned the key in the ignition. As they drove away she saw, in her rear view mirror, that Carol and the man had gone inside the bungalow.

'What did you make of all that?' Norma asked, then carried on before Rose could answer. 'Like I said before, something's not right there. I've never met him, but I'm certain that man isn't her husband. And what did she mean about Beth? You don't think she's . . .' but she couldn't bring herself to put it into words.

Rose knew that the questions had been

rhetorical. This was a trait Norma shared with Doreen Clarke. It was merely the voicing of thoughts to try to make some sense of them.

Spoken aloud, what Norma had suggested sounded ridiculous, but the idea had passed through Rose's mind, too. And, reminiscent of the Bradley twins, there seemed to be no love lost between the sisters.

'This'll do me. Pull in anywhere it's safe to park,' Norma said when they reached the tiny square in Marazion. 'I'll walk from here to the churchyard. I don't know about you, but I need a bit of fresh air now. Thanks for the lift, dear. And like I said before, you're always welcome.'

Rose smiled, wondering if Norma was a little lonely now that she had no family left at home. She could do with some fresh air herself and the car would be all right where it was. She got out and locked it then walked down the short alleyway between two buildings, which led to the beach. This was where it happened, she thought. The scene was once more vivid in her mind. There was no question that the child had gone willingly; she could almost see her smile. But something about the scene she was visualising didn't quite fit. She sat on the fine sand where it was dry because the tide did not come in that far and tried to work out what was puzzling her. Was it something someone had said?

She found it difficult to concentrate because her artist's eye kept observing the people who were walking past. The beach was a popular place for walkers and those exercising their dogs, especially on a weekend morning when the clarity of the air was unbelievably startling. There were a few small puffs of white cloud in an otherwise blue sky and the shades of the sea were varied. On the horizon it was a translucent green where the rays of the sun shone down. Where rocks were concealed beneath its surface it was tinged with purple and closer to the shore it was aquamarine edged with white spume.

The tide was still going out. At the edge of the water were flocks of gulls; mainly the ubiquitous herring gulls but also the smaller blockheaded gulls with their red legs and beaks and the small dark smudge behind each eye; their winter plumage. In the summer they would sport a chocolate hood. In the distance were a few of the far larger, solitary blackbacked variety.

Although the wind no longer blew from the east it was still too chilly to sit still for long. Rose stood up, brushed the sand from her skirt and strode along the beach.

Around the curve of the coastline, along which

the Penzance to Paddington railway line ran, she could see the walls of Penzance harbour and the tower of the church of St Mary the Virgin which was a familiar landmark to locals and could be seen from many viewpoints around the bay. Beyond that lay Newlyn with its steep tiers of granite properties, and the road to Mousehole where her house stood. She could just make it out.

Fifteen minutes later she had reached one of the wide streams which dissected the beach, running from the hills through tunnels over which the road had been built. Her shoes would be ruined if she tried to cross it. On a warmer day she would have taken them off and waded to the other side. Now, she retraced her steps, warm from the exercise. Her shoes left deeper imprints in the more gravely texture of the sand closer to the shore. By the time she got back to the car her calves were beginning to ache. Walking in sand was much harder than on grass or a pavement. But her mind was no clearer. Don't think about it and whatever it was will come back to you, she told herself as she began the short drive home.

Just over an hour later, Jack arrived in Marazion. With plenty of time to spare he had stopped for a few bits of shopping and bought the local paper, the *Sunday Independent*, which covered the three West Country counties. As he was early he would have a chance to read it.

The Godolphin Arms was a large pub with a separate dining room, a children's play area and panoramic views over the bay. Sunday lunches were already being served. Jack ordered coffee and chose a seat at a table in the window.

He recalled one other occasion when he had been there with Rose. They had watched a constant stream of visitors returning from the Mount, most of them unaware of the vagaries of the tide. The majority had made it back but a few stragglers remained on the causeway not realising that the sea would swirl in ahead of them. There was slimy seaweed on parts of the causeway and the stones were uneven so it was far too dangerous to run. They had simply had to wade, shoes and jeans becoming soaked. One strong young man had hefted his girlfriend onto his shoulders and piggybacked her to dry land.

To their astonishment they had seen one couple attempt to make it out to the Mount but they soon had to turn back. Today no one was on the causeway; it was hardly visible. There was another hour and a half before low water.

Jack opened the paper. As he had expected there was coverage of Beth's disappearance but the article only reiterated what had been reported in the daily press, along with the number to ring if anyone had any relevant information.

There had been callers, there always were, and each one had to be taken seriously even though there were claims that the person could predict where Beth was or could swear that she had been abducted by aliens. There was always the chance of a double bluff, that the person at the end of the line really did have information but was tying to prove they were more clever than the police. 'Inspector Pearce?'

Jack looked up. He had given Poole a description of himself but he would have been recognised anyway as at the moment he was the only single male in the room. The man standing beside him was as tall as Jack but that was the only similarity. Michael Poole possessed typical Anglo-Saxon looks; blond hair and blue eyes and skin which looked as if it would burn rather than tan. Jack recognised that he would normally be considered good-looking by women, but that day he looked exhausted.

Jack stood and shook his hand. This was an informal chat, not an interview. 'Can I get you a drink?'

Michael hesitated, unsure if this was some sort of test. He had the car, after all. 'Thank you. A pint of bitter, please.'

Jack went to the bar to buy it then returned to the table. There were more customers now; he wondered just how private their talk would be. However, the couples and family groups all seemed engrossed in their own conversations.

'Thank you.' Michael took a sip of his beer then placed the glass on the table in a way which suggested he hadn't really wanted a drink. No doubt he was nervous. 'I know there's no further news,' he began. 'I was at Sally's place this morning and an officer rang to say so.' He looked at Jack, hoping that he was wrong, hoping that in the time since he had left her something may have happened. But Jack's grim expression gave him the answer.

'You do realise that everything that can be done is being done.' Banal, meaningless words but they needed to be spoken.

Michael frowned as he nodded, wondering what exactly it was that they were doing.

'Why did you and Sally decide to part?'

'It was not my decision. I loved her, I still love her, but she didn't want to stay with me.'

'Was this before or after Beth was born?'

'Before. She can't have been more than a couple of months pregnant when she left. At the time I thought she might have been using me, that a baby was all she wanted.' He shrugged in resignation. 'If so, she certainly fooled me.'

'This is going to sound impertinent, but I need to ask you about your maintenance arrangements.'

'What?' Michael had picked up his glass. He replaced it on the table without drinking from it. His hand, Jack noticed, was shaking.

'We happen to know that you have continued to make them, despite the situation. Some men wouldn't have. You see, you told us that you didn't know where she was living and we happen to know that she doesn't have a bank account.' In Cornwall, not having one was not as unusual as it would have been anywhere else.

He hesitated as he thought about his method of doing so. 'You're right. Sally didn't want me to know where she was living. I saw Beth a couple of times when she brought her up to Looe when she was a baby. At first I was angry because I didn't get to see her more often, but I respected Sally's wishes. I even insisted on a blood test to prove the baby was mine. Anyway, Sally continued to refuse to give me her address. Alice wouldn't either, although I knew she wanted to. We came to an arrangement, I was to give the money to Alice on a monthly basis and she would forward it on.'

'Have you ever seen Beth's birth certificate.'

'No. Why?'

'I just wondered if you were named on it as the father. Look, the payments you made, was the amount fixed by the court or any other legal body?'

'No. We worked out a sum that seemed fair and I've stuck to it. My own living expenses aren't great. I intend on increasing the amount when Beth . . .' *Gets older,* he had been about to say. But there was no guarantee she would ever do so.

Jack's coffee was cold and had been for some time. He asked a passing waiter if he could bring him some more.

'Not for me,' Michael said when Jack indicated his glass. He had hardly touched the beer.

They were silent for several minutes. It was Michael who decided to speak first. 'I have a good idea why you wanted to see me and, although I can't expect you to believe me, I love Beth dearly. I would never do anything to harm that little girl.'

He seemed sincere and Jack felt inclined to believe him. At least he now had an impression of Poole. 'Is there anything else which has come to mind which might help us in our enquiries? I know you've already been questioned but you've had time to think now.'

'There is something else; although I'm sure it can't possibly be relevant.' He shook his head in denial. 'I do happen to know that no one else has mentioned it.'

Jack was fully alert. Something else. And how did Poole know that no one had mentioned it unless he had taken the trouble to ask. And what reason would he have had for asking? This was going to be more important than the man realised. Jack waited, fearing that to push him might make him change his mind.

'I had an affair with Carol, this was before Sally and I lived together. Oh, don't get me wrong, Carol wasn't married at that time. We were together for about a year but it didn't work out. Carol . . . well, to be honest, she was jealous of every woman I spoke to and she kept trying to change me. Anyway we split up but I still saw Alice, that's her mother, quite often. We've always got on well, she's a decent woman. That's when I started to get to know Sally – she was visiting her mother when we met. I thought we were ideally suited. She had all of Carol's qualities but without the jealous streak. It only went wrong when she became pregnant.

'At the time I didn't know she was expecting a baby. She moved down here and only told me after Beth was born. It was such an odd thing to do.'

'Perhaps she thought you'd want her to have an abortion or that you'd believe she was trying to trap you.'

Michael laughed mirthlessly. 'Trap me? I'd spent ages begging her to marry me. Believe me, Inspector, I wanted to be trapped.'

'And you later applied for custody. Why was that?'

He flushed. 'There were two reasons, and I'm not proud of my motives. Firstly I thought it would shock her into coming back to me, which I later realised was no basis upon which to build a relationship.'

'And secondly?'

'Carol had recently been in touch with me. She rang to say that Sally wasn't looking after Beth properly and, to be frank, she accused her of being an alcoholic.'

'And you believed her?'

'It was a possibility. Sally always did enjoy a drink. I wondered if the stress of being a single mother had tipped her over the edge.'

'Enough to harm Beth?'

'Good God, no. Besides why should she do so now? Surely it's only when they're babies that mothers do such things. And Beth would have been starting school soon.'

Would have been. Poole had previously talked of his daughter in the present tense. Had he come to accept that Beth was dead, or did he know for a fact that she was? But he had a point. Severe postnatal depression could cause a woman to harm her child, as could the continuous high-pitched screams of an infant. 'What was Carol like when you first knew her?'

'In what way?' Michael was surprised at the change of tack and couldn't see where any of the questions were leading. He had come prepared to lay bare his own life, not his ex-girlfriend's.

'Was she easygoing, for instance?' Jack was recalling Rose's words about Carol being obsessive. Obsessive people could also be tipped over the edge.

'Yes, she was. She enjoyed life. As I said, the only problem was her jealousy. Not just over other women, although she had no cause to be, it involved anyone who took my attention away from her.'

So the seeds were there all those years ago. And then, when Michael moved in with her sister, and her sister subsequently had a child by him, how did she feel then? But it came back to the same thing, why wait for more than four years to do anything about it? 'I won't detain you any longer, Mr Poole, unless you can think of anything else.'

Michael glanced out of the window before meeting Jack' eyes. 'No, there's nothing else,' he said. It was then that Jack knew he was lying.

CHAPTER TEN

Neither Rose nor Norma had met Carol's husband but they both knew that he was away. It was too late to worry about what they thought of a man visiting her when she was at home alone. Marcus was there, she couldn't make him disappear. From the way in which he was dressed and the model of his car which was new, they would have guessed that he was not a workman of some sort even if it had not been a Sunday. 'You'd better come in,' she said to him ungraciously.

He followed her to the kitchen where she immediately began washing the tea and coffee things.

'I apologise for just turning up like this but I

couldn't wait until this afternoon. I need to know, Carol, and I need to know now exactly where I stand. You know I'm perfectly willing to take on the children and treat them as my own, if that's what worrying you. We'll cope. I'll do whatever's necessary to make the three of you happy.'

Carol stood, her head bowed, her hands in their rubber gloves immersed in the soapy water. Her dark hair had fallen forward and hid her face. She blinked and realised that she was crying, that her tears were hitting the suds and making the bubbles burst. I must have been mad, she thought. I've used Marcus to play a stupid, immature game that was never going to work and now its backfired. I just needed to prove I was lovable and now I'm about to hurt him badly. All right, John seemed to have lost whatever appeal he had held for her, but maybe that was because he was away so much; more often than he was at home, in fact, and they didn't get a chance to settle down together when he was at home. There always seemed so many other things to do rather than work at their relationship. He had taken the job in Saudi only because he wanted to provide well for his family. He was a good man, he didn't deserve what she had done to him; done to him twice, even though he was not aware of it. It was time she grew up and took responsibility for her life. Had she done so in the first place things would have been so very different.

She turned to face Marcus. 'I've made up my mind. I can't see you any more.' He flinched and his face paled. 'I'm very sorry, Marcus, truly I am. I've enjoyed what we had but it's over. If you do tell John then it's no more than I deserve and I'm prepared to take the consequences.'

'I never intended telling him, Carol.' He saw his mistake. The threat of blackmail was hardly conducive to a love affair, to persuading a woman to leave her husband and come and live with you. 'I'll go now. I promise I won't bother you again. All I can do is to wish you luck.' He kissed her on the cheek and let himself out. It was some minutes before he was able to drive away.

Carol sat at the kitchen table, the dishes unheeded now. She was shuddering with sobs: for Marcus, for John, for herself, but most of all for Beth. She had done what she ought to have done some time ago but she felt no real relief. She despised herself for all the bad she had done, the pain she had caused and was now causing herself. One admission is all it would have taken and her whole life would have been different. It was too late now, the damage was done.

She walked slowly to the bathroom where she washed her face and renewed her makeup. She would collect the children early. All she wanted was to hold their small warm bodies in her arms and smell their familiar scent.

And I'll telephone Geoff Carter, too, she decided as she went out to the car. I'll apologise for dragging him into my mess and thank him for his generosity with his time but I won't see him again. There would be no more complications.

Carol felt she had reached a milestone. It was the most optimistic she had felt for some time. If only it wasn't for Beth. Tears filled her eyes again. She brushed them away hastily because if she started crying in earnest she would not be able to see to drive.

Rose had finished weeding the garden and had spent the afternoon reading, which was a rare treat. At six thirty she was in the kitchen deciding what to cook for supper. There was a glass of wine at hand. The choice was between red mullet and squid; either would take only a few minutes to cook. The vegetables were already in saucepans. I'll ring Dad and see how he got on in Redruth and then I'll decide, she thought as she carried her wine glass into the sitting-room. She almost dropped it when, just as she reached for the receiver, the telephone rang. 'Rose? Are you okay?'

For a second she didn't recognise Laura's voice, she was normally so bubbly unless she'd had one of her many rows with Trevor. This sounded different. 'Yes, of course I am. Why?'

'God, you haven't heard.'

'Heard what?' In that instant she understood what was meant by the phrase of one's stomach turning over. She knew what was coming but prayed she was wrong.

'They've found her. They've found Beth.' But not alive, Rose knew that from Laura's tone. Still she had to ask.

'Alive?'

'No.'

Rose inhaled deeply. She had seen Beth once, and then only for a very short time. If she felt like this, how on earth must those close to her be feeling? 'How do you know?'

'It was on the local news. They didn't say it was her, just that the body of a child had been discovered somewhere several miles the other side of Marazion. It was well hidden, apparently. And it was the usual story, a dog walker found her. Well, the dog did. I'm so sorry, Rose. Would you like me to come over?'

214

'Yes. Yes, I would.'

'I'll be there as soon as I can.'

Rose replaced the receiver. Her meal was forgotten. She should have known that after all this time it was unlikely that Beth would be found alive, she had told herself so time and again but there had always been that grain of hope, the no news is good news point of view. Impossible to ring Sally now but some time in the future she would go and see her, and maybe Carol, too.

She was still standing beside the small table which held the telephone when it rang again. This time it was Geoff Carter; he, too, had heard the news. 'It makes me feel sick. I know what I'd do to the person who did this,' he said furiously. 'And now I don't know what to do. Do you think I ought to ring Carol, or even go and see her? She was in such a state before I don't know what this is going to do to her.'

'I think it's best to leave it for the minute, Geoff.' Rose guessed that all the family would be questioned again this time in even more depth. And if Carol had had any part in the murder then it would be unwise for Geoff to become further involved.

'You're probably right, but I can't help worrying about her, especially as she's on her own.'

'She won't be. She's picking her children up tonight.' Rose wondered if she knew yet. But she would, of course. The police may not have released a name but they wouldn't have released any sort of statement if the family didn't know. Otherwise what worse way could there be to hear about the death of a child than over the radio?

'I'll be in touch.' Geoff said goodbye and hung up.

Within the next few minutes both Barry and her father telephoned. She was grateful for their concern but needed a few minutes for the news to sink in. When Laura arrived, clutching a bottle of wine which she had bought at the Coop on her way through Newlyn, Rose was in tears.

Laura put the bottle on the kitchen table and hugged her wordlessly. She knew what her friend was thinking, that she was torn in two, half of her wishing she had never been on the beach that day because she would have been less emotionally involved, the other half believing she could have done something to prevent it. 'Get it out of your system, as my mother used to say.' She handed Rose a tissue from the box she kept on top of the fridge.

'I'm sorry, it's not like me to cry.'

It wasn't. In all the years they had known each

other Laura had rarely seen her do so except after David died and, more recently, at her mother's funeral. 'I'll open this, it'll do us both good.'

Rose sat down. She suddenly felt very tired. 'I saw the sister today, Carol. She and Sally had had a row. She must feel terrible about that now.'

'And you're feeling terrible, too. I know you, Rose. But this time you really couldn't do anything, you're just going to have to accept that.'

Rose smiled wanly as Laura stood, bent over, with the bottle between her knees and tugged at the cork. It came out of the bottle with a single heave. Laura's long, curly hair, scrunched up in a bright red, frilly band, swung as she stood upright. 'You're right,' Rose said.

'Here, drink this. It's Rioja. You'll like it. It was on offer in the Co-op.' Laura poured two glasses and sat down. She crossed her long, thin legs, which, today, were encased in harlequin patterned leggings. Her long sweatshirt was fluorescent pink. Only Laura could get away with wearing such clothes.

'Thanks.' Rose picked up her wine and took a sip. 'You're right, it's very nice. I think I'll buy some myself.'

'Has Jack been in touch with you today?'

'No. I've hardly spoken to him lately. He'll be very busy now, though. Likewise, Barry. He's spending a lot of time with Jenny.'

'Good for him. He's spent far too many years mooning around over you.'

'Very funny. Anyway, what you were saying, Laura, about the Bradley twins. I'm sure there's something similar going on between Sally and her sister.' She related what she had heard of the row and Carol's comments later on that morning. 'And Geoff Carter seems to think that Carol's, well, unbalanced in some way.'

'Geoff Carter? Good God, woman, where on earth does he fit into all this?'

Rose explained how they had met and what had followed afterwards.

Laura snorted. 'That's bloody typical. If there's any chance of that man getting his leg over, he won't waste it.'

'I don't think it was like that.'

Laura raised an eyebrow in disbelief. 'I see. Anyway, you're now convinced that this Carol who, according to what you've told me, is obsessive, unbalanced, jealous of her sister and man mad, has murdered her sister's child.'

Rose didn't answer. She was chewing her thumb nail, deep in thought.

'Well, if she really is all those things, it's possible, I suppose. Rose? Are you with me?'

'Yes. I was listening.'

They both looked up when they heard a car pulling into the driveway, its headlights illuminating the shed and turning the grass a peculiar shade of blue.

'It's Barry. I'd know the sound of that engine anywhere,' Rose said as she got up to open the door. 'Hello, I thought you and Jenny were going out.'

'We were. I mean, we did. We spent the day at the Eden Project. You really must take Arthur there, he'll love it. You should see the variety of plants and those dome things are amazing. Hi, there, Laura.'

'Hi, there, yourself. If you get a glass you can help yourself to some wine.'

'Thanks. Just a small one.'

Laura grinned. Some things would never change. Barry would not risk even one full unit of alcohol when he had the car.

He sat down. 'I had to come, Rose, but I didn't realise you already had company. I know how upset you must be.'

'Company? Me? I'm just part of the furniture, dear. And there's nothing like having a manly shoulder to cry on.' Laura poured his wine.

Barry removed his glasses and polished them with the hem of his sweater before replacing them immediately. During all the years the two women had known him he had always worn glasses. If his prescription had changed, his taste in frames had not. They were always the sort of plastic that looks like tortoiseshell. Without them his face had a naked vulnerability. 'That's why I'm here. Are you really all right, Rosie?'

'Yes, I am now. It was such a shock even though I was sort of expecting it.'

'Jack'll have his work cut out now. Oh, damn.' As he'd picked up his glass his elbow knocked against the edge of the table and red wine splashed over his sleeve. 'My new jacket,' he complained as if it was someone else's fault.

Rose had noticed how smart he looked, how, lately, his clothes matched and he no longer wore the V-necked jumpers with threadbare elbows. Tonight, shirt, sweater, trousers and jacket were all in shades of autumnal browns and tans. She got up to fetch him a damp dishcloth. 'It probably won't show,' she said as she handed it to him, 'and, besides . . .' She stopped. New jacket. That's what it was, that's what had been at the back of her mind since this morning. She would decide what to do about it later. It was certainly not something which could be ignored.

'Well,' Laura said, 'as we're all at a bit of a loose end, why don't we adjourn to the pub?'

Barry smiled at her. 'Well, now, that'll make a real change, Laura, won't it? Mind you, your friend here is just as bad.'

Until he'd met Jenny, Barry had always been a solitary man, quite contented with his own company. Consequently, what he'd never been able to understand was that for Rose, living and working alone, and Laura, when Trevor was at sea, their individual or joint excursions to the pub were for socialising rather than drinking, although they did enjoy the latter too.

The wind still blew as they got into Barry's car, but it was more gentle now, with a hint of rain. A veil of mist hung over the horizon. It shrouded the top of St Michael's Mount and blurred the numerous lights on the salvage tug.

'Shall we go to the Tolcarne for a change?' Barry suggested.

'As long as they sell alcohol we don't care,' Laura said, playing up to the image Barry had created.

He parked outside and they all went in. Barry had to stoop beneath the lintel of the door of the low-ceilinged pub.

To their left was the dining area, to the right the narrow bar where jazz was played twice a week.

There was room to sit in one of the window recesses. Laura and Rose sat down whilst Barry bought their drinks; wine for his guests, mineral water for himself.

'Is it serious with Jenny?' It was Laura who asked. She had wanted to know for several weeks but she had not had the opportunity to talk to him.

'We're not sure yet. We're fine as we are at the moment.' He did not want to talk about it, personal matters always embarrassed him. All he had wanted to do was to take Rose's mind off the tragedy and any further part she might wish to take in it. He had not expected to see Laura or to end up in the pub.

At nine thirty they went their separate ways, Barry in the car, Rose and Laura on foot because they had refused his offer of a lift.

As an inspector, especially being the one already in charge of the case, Jack was responsible for organising things at the scene of the crime; the second crime; no longer abduction, but murder.

On that bright Sunday morning Jacko Tonkin

had been walking his dog. He lived in the centre of Marazion where it was impossible to let Benji off the lead. He had retired almost five years ago, by then already a widower, and driving out to the countryside where Benji could run free, gave him something to do.

Jacko was fit for his seventy years and the dog helped him keep that way. Together they had discovered a footpath which crossed two fields and wound through some woodland. 'What's he found now?' Jacko muttered as Benji began rooting around some distance off the footpath. When called, Benji, usually so obedient, failed to respond to his master. Still muttering crossly, Jacko went in after him; brambles, denuded of their fruit and foliage, tore at his clothing.

He was about to reach for the dog's collar but what he saw sent him staggering backwards. Beneath the tangle of the undergrowth was the decomposing body of a child. He steadied himself against the trunk of a tree as he first retched, then vomited, splashing his shoes in the process.

With a great effort of will he fastened Benji's lead and dragged him away. Not taking his eyes off the spot he used the mobile phone his daughter had given him last Christmas, insisting he didn't go out without it, and rang the police.

It seemed an age until they arrived, two men tramping along the path, although they had had to do as he had done and park in the layby before walking the rest of the way. When Jacko looked at his watch it had, in fact, been no more than twenty minutes.

Trembling, he told them what Benji had found, then he pointed with a shaking finger towards where the body lay. Benji growled as the two men approached the spot.

Like himself, one of the officers vomited. He was young, it might have been the first time he had faced death, at least in that form.

An hour later Jacko was back in his house sitting by the fire, sipping hot, sweet tea laced with brandy. A policeman was with him to make sure he was all right as he had refused to go to hospital to be assessed for shock. In the morning he would be required to make a statement, but he wasn't up to it yet.

Without being told, he knew exactly who the person was that Benji had inadvertently found.

By the time Jack arrived the arc lamps were in position and a tent had been erected over the place where Beth Jones lay. Only when the officers had reported back had he arranged for the members of the serious crime team to be despatched to the spot. It would have been a total waste of time and money if the call had been a hoax.

What Jack saw sickened him but his stomach did not let him down. And at least they were fortunate in that there were no onlookers, no passing people needing to be moved on.

It was dark by the time they had packed up. By then Jack realised that there was no way in which the mother could be asked to identify the child. The clothes would have to suffice because both the natural consequences of death and nature, in the form of foxes or rats, had taken their course. Clothes and a detailed dental comparison, Jack thought as they made their way back to their various vehicles.

Sally Jones and her mother were accompanied to the hospital mortuary. The child's clothes, not too badly damaged, were laid out on a table in plastic evidence bags. Sally took one look at them and fainted. No one was able to catch her before she fell to the floor. Alice Jones was bent double, her face in her hands.

Someone must have taken them home but it was a journey they could not remember. Once more a female officer remained with them, making them tea and encouraging them to talk through their grief.

Yet another night passed without sleep in that household. Sally knew that both Carol and Michael had been informed but neither of them made contact. It was just as well; she wouldn't have been able to bear to speak to them.

Back at the station in Camborne, Jack had sent someone to break the news to Michael Poole and Carol Harte, then he set the paperwork in motion. Once that was done he sat in his chair and thought over all that had happened. The Home Office pathologist estimated that Beth had been dead for at least four days, possibly even five, which meant that she was killed immediately after she was taken from the beach. From his initial examination it appeared that no sexual motive was involved; the post mortem would tell them for certain. Would that be a comfort to her parents? He could only hope so. As yet, the identification could not be taken for granted, although Jack had little doubt that the child was Beth. Murderers did change their victims' clothes and any other forms of identification, but in this case it seemed highly unlikely, especially as no other child was on their books as missing. The hair is hers, Jack thought, the long, dark hair of the photograph that Sally had provided, the same colour her mother's would have been had she not dyed it blonde.

He had already roused the dentist who had promised to go straight to his surgery for Beth's notes. 'Do you want me to deliver them to you?' he had asked, surprising Jack with his willingness, even eagerness to help.

'If you don't mind. We'd be very grateful.' They would be on hand ready for the post mortem which had been scheduled for the morning.

There was nothing more that could be done that night. In the morning, in daylight and when a little of the shock had worn off, the interviews would begin again. But where to go with them? The only difference now, horrendous as it was, was that Beth was dead. Nothing they did could bring her back. What more can we do that we haven't done already, Jack asked himself as he switched off the light and left the building.

He felt dirty and in need of a long scalding shower and a stiff drink, but more than that he wanted to see Rose.

He drove straight to her house. No longer tired, but fuelled by adrenalin, he needed to talk.

The roads were busier than he had anticipated and approaching headlights flashed past him at regular intervals. On the more brightly lit outskirts of Penzance he wound down his window and let the chill air wash over him. He began to feel less stale.

Driving along the Promenade he could smell the sea, a smell he had known all his life apart from the short time he had lived in Leeds, where he had transferred to gain experience; a time when he learnt that he could never be happy anywhere other than Cornwall. He had persuaded Marian, his then wife, to move back down with him, but the same had applied in reverse. They were divorced not long after she returned to Leeds. It was all quite amicable; they simply realised that they wanted different things from life. The boys, men now, had spent a great deal of their holidays with Jack and both were keen surfers. He smiled as he recalled how, on his last visit, Daniel had proclaimed that Rose was 'a bit of all right'.

As he changed gear to turn the sharp corner into Rose's drive he was relieved to see that the lights were on. Good. Rose was at home.

'I've seen it all before, Trevor,' Laura commented as she made him a sandwich for supper. They had eaten earlier but Trevor had been working on the boat and was hungry again. The small gold cross he wore in his ear glinted beneath the kitchen spotlights, revealed only when he pushed back his hair which rested on the collar of his thick, checked shirt.

'Seen what before?' he asked without raising his head from the newspaper.

'Don't you ever listen to anything I say?'

He put the newspaper down and saw his wife's shoulders jerking as she sliced his sandwich in two. The danger signs were all too familiar. He had better pay attention now. 'Of course I do. This, I assume, has to be to do with Rose.' He reached out and slapped her on the bottom, but only gently.

She turned to him and smiled. The danger was over, another row had been averted. 'Yes. It's bad enough that she saw that little girl taken from her mother, how's she going to feel now?'

Trevor understood what Laura meant. He knew Rose as well as anyone could know another person who did not share his house. She would feel responsible and guilty without reason, that was how she was. And this was what was bothering his wife. Rose would desperately want to make amends and would probably end up in trouble by doing so. 'You can't stop her, Laura, you know that as well as I do.'

'I realise that, but do you think it would be a good idea to forewarn Jack?'

'No. I don't. He'll have enough on his plate at the moment and you know what he's like where Rose is concerned. He doesn't need the extra worry right now, he won't be able to concentrate if he's wondering what Rose is going to be doing next.'

'You're right.' She kissed the top of his head as she handed him his sandwich.

Trevor felt it was safe to return to the newspaper.

Laura, sitting opposite him was deep in thought as she sipped her tea. 'I'm off to bed,' she said ten minutes later. 'Have you finished with the teapot?'

He nodded, grinning, as she picked it up and emptied it down the sink. 'But I haven't finished with you, maid. Get up those stairs and get your kit off, woman. I'll be right behind you.'

'Honestly, you don't ever change.'

'And aren't you glad of that,' he responded with another grin as he put an arm around her shoulder and they went upstairs together.

'I know it's late, Jack, but there's something you should know. Can you ring me, or come over, if possible. It's about Tuesday, I think it's important.' Rose hung up. She had telephoned twice before but had not left a message and she didn't want to ring him at Camborne, knowing it would be hectic there.

Half an hour later his car pulled into the drive. She hurried to the kitchen to let him in. Before she could speak he pulled her to him and held her closely. 'What a hell of a day,' he said, as he breathed in the scent of her hair; lemon shampoo with a hint of smoke from one of her rationed cigarettes.

'I'm glad you got the message. I think it really is important.'

He took a step backwards and stared at her uncomprehendingly. 'What message?'

'I left one for you at the flat. I thought that was why you're here.'

'No. I haven't been home. I just wanted to see you.'

She took in his tired face. 'Shall I make us some tea?'

'No, a stiff drink's what I need.'

She poured whisky for him, adding two lumps of ice, as he liked it, and wine for herself. They went through to the sitting-room where it was warmer and more comfortable.

'Tell me the worst,' Jack said once they were seated.

'I saw Norma today and she told me something, quite inadvertently, that didn't fit in with what I saw.'

'Go on.' He leant forward knowing that whatever she said it would be important. Rose was a reliable witness and didn't miss much.

'I remember thinking at the time, when Beth went off with that man, that she was far too skimpily dressed for the weather. Well, this morning Norma said that when she last saw Beth it was on Tuesday morning. She was going out of the house with Sally and she was wearing her new jacket. The thing is, Jack, she wasn't wearing it when I saw her and Sally didn't have it with her. All she had was her handbag. When I saw Beth she was wearing jeans, a shirt and a woollen top.'

Jack frowned. Perhaps Beth had been running around and was hot, the coat removed and lying forgotten on the beach, forgotten because of what had happened next. No, that was impossible, the beach had been searched. 'But she was wearing it when we found her.'

'How odd. So in that case, where was it?'

Jack thought about it for several minutes. One explanation came to mind. 'If someone gave them a lift down to the beach, the coat may have been left in the car. Whoever dropped them off parked, then walked down and took Beth. Now Beth either knows who he is or recognises him because of the lift so she goes off with him willingly. Then, either before or after he's killed her, he puts her coat back on. He obviously can't afford to be found in possession of it.' He shrugged. It was a weak explanation but the best he could come up with. Deep down he didn't actually think it had happened that way. No one, including Sally, had mentioned them getting a lift, but maybe it hadn't been considered important.

'I suppose, it's possible, but what mother would leave a child's coat behind on a day like that?'

'It depends upon the mother.'

'Yes.' They were both thinking the same thing. If Carol's account of her sister had any grain of truth in it, if Sally truly was an unfit mother, then it could easily have been overlooked.

Rose went on to explain her theory about sibling rivalry. Jack listened carefully. If, under such circumstances, the two women had rowed then it might be as serious as Rose was suggesting.

'And another thing, Carol has a boyfriend. You don't think he might be involved, do you? I mean, Beth could have met him at some point.'

'Boyfriend? How the hell do you find these things out?'

Rose blushed. She did not want to involve Geoff Carter if it could be avoided.

'Is there anything else you're holding back?'

'I wasn't holding back, as you put it, so there's no need for sarcasm. I only remembered what Norma told me this evening and until I saw him myself the question of the boyfriend was only hearsay. Carol could have lied to Geoff, to gain attention, or to feed her obsession or for any number of reasons.' Too late, Rose realised what she had just said. Jack was smiling.

'Ah, Geoff Carter. So he's been sniffing around there, too.'

'Not this time. This was different.'

'If you say so. Anyway, you were saying, you saw the boyfriend.'

She nodded, knowing she was about to add fuel to the fire. 'We were at Carol's bungalow. I'd gone to see Sally, to see if there was anything I could do and Norma was just on her way out. We heard part of the quarrel and I decided it was best not to go up. Within seconds Michael Poole came down the stairs and then, very soon afterwards, Carol did. She invited us to her place for coffee.'

And you would not have been able to resist that under any circumstances, Jack thought. It was amazing – within a few days Rose had met the whole damn cast. Not only that, she had discovered the existence of a boyfriend that the police did not know about, another male, another possible suspect, especially if Rose's suspicions of jealousy were correct. But that, of course, was Rose. Yet how innocent she looked, how small, in her armchair by the fire with her reddish auburn hair shining and her face bereft of makeup. 'It's too late to do anything more tonight,' he said. But first thing in the morning he would be interviewing Carol Harte in depth and then her boyfriend, whoever he might be. And, cruel though it might be, Sally would have to be questioned about the matter of her daughter's coat. 'Jack?'

'I'm sorry, I was thinking.'

'I asked if you'd eaten.'

He couldn't recall how many hours ago it was that he'd had a sandwich but it was probably more than seven.

'I can see that the answer is no. I'll get you something. Help yourself to another drink.' She sent to the kitchen and made a mushroom omelette whilst a baguette warmed in the oven. But when she carried the tray into the sitting-room, Jack was asleep in the chair.

CHAPTER ELEVEN

When Geoff Carter opened the gallery on Monday morning he was surprised to find there was a telephone message. His machine timed it as having been left at ten past three the previous afternoon. Now and then a potential overseas buyer rang after hours, but this was no customer. She had rung before she received the awful news.

'Hello, it's Carol Harte,' the voice began tentatively. 'We met in Tesco's.' Geoff shook his head. Was she that insecure she thought he'd have forgotten her already? 'I just wanted to thank you for your time and your kindness to me on Friday night. Talking to you helped so much that I've been able to sort out my problems.' There was a slight pause. 'I, well, your offer was very generous but I won't need a shoulder to cry on again. Thank you, Geoff. And goodbye.'

'There goes another one. At least it was a polite brush off,' he said to himself as he began to prepare the gallery for the day ahead. And what a day it was; an Indian summer day. Hopefully it would bring the customers out.

By mid-morning he had already made two sales and was delighted further by the third because it was one of Rose's dramatic oils. She, of course, would be even more delighted. When the customer had left he rang her to give her the news but she wasn't at home. He ought to have realised that she would be making the most of the fine weather and working out of doors somewhere. He left a message then added, 'By the way, our mutual friend Carol Harte rang me to say that she's sorted out her problems in the short time since I spoke to her. I wonder what she finally decided.' The last sentence was spoken deliberately. He didn't know the answer but he would bet anything that Rose would try to find it out. He turned his attention to the coffee which had finally percolated. It was the second pot he had made that day. Good business always made him thirsty.

* * *

Jack had gone by the time Rose got up on Monday morning. He must have woken very early as the clock on the mantelpiece showed it was still only 6.21. She had tucked a duvet around him where he slept in the chair, knowing that if she woke him he would not go back to sleep again. He was the only person she had met who could sleep anywhere and not wake feeling stiff or unrefreshed. He had left a note saying he would call in later and let her know the outcome of his enquiries about Beth's jacket.

She wasted no time that morning and was out of the house by nine thirty. It would have been sooner but she had waited until it was completely light and could gauge the weather better.

It was some time since she had painted a mine stack and that was what her objective was today, or, at least, to make a start. There was a scene nearby she had not attempted before.

She drove out of Penzance and along the A394 until she reached Goldsithney, a village on the other side of Marazion. She parked on the grass verge of the road and walked to a good vantage point where she scanned the landscape carefully. In the foreground was a field which had been harvested earlier in the year. She could work from there without fear of damaging any crops or unsettling animals. Beyond the field was a hedge, behind that and to the right was an old engine house, not, like many, in ruins but complete with slate roof and mellow brickwork that was not even starting to crumble. There was also a house, half hidden by a tall tree, and two mine stacks, also in good condition. These structures gave perfect balance to the scene, as did the colours. A blue sky arced over the earthy, autumnal tints of nature and the buildings. Relief was added in the form of the white walls of the partially visible house.

Within ten minutes Rose had planned the painting in her head. She chose a spot to stand, opened her canvas satchel and set up her easel and the canvas she had prepared in advance then began to block it out.

Stopping only once for coffee she had brought in a flask, she carried on until her back began to ache. It was time to stop anyway as the light had started to change. The sky was paler, milky now rather than blue, and there was a haze building up in the distance. She packed up her things and walked back to the car.

On the way home she decided to call in and see her father. They had not made plans to meet again when they last spoke over the telephone and she didn't want him to feel neglected. There was also the matter of inviting Jack for Christmas. When other things, such as Beth Jones, preoccupied her, her memory for everyday things became impaired. And the cake remained unmade although she had got as far as putting the fruit in brandy to soak.

'What a lovely surprise,' Arthur said when he answered the door. 'Come in, I'm only watching the racing.' He had always taken an interest in horses and read the form but since his retirement he had been able to attend meetings as well as watching the runners on television. He and Evelyn had always loved the Cheltenham meeting in March. But there were no racecourses in Cornwall, only point-to-point meetings. The nearest racing was in Devon, at Newton Abbot or Exeter.

'I won't spoil your fun, then. I just wanted to know when you'd like to come over for dinner.'

'How about Thursday? I'm busy tomorrow and you've got your class on Wednesday.'

'Oh? And why are you smiling so enigmatically?' He can't have met a woman, not yet, Rose thought with a touch of panic followed by a surge of loyalty to her mother. They had had a long and happy marriage and Arthur had adored Evelyn. But that, Rose realised, meant nothing, because she had seen it before. In similar circumstances the bereaved partner often found someone else quickly. Having experienced a happy relationship they were eager to repeat the pattern.

'Sid, that's my friend in Redruth, has suggested that I go along with him to bridge classes. Apparently, once you know what you're doing you get invited to bridge parties. It's an ideal way in which to get to know a few more people.'

'It's a wonderful idea.' She hugged him, partly in relief but also because she was genuinely pleased. 'Now, while I'm here, there's something I want to ask you. It's about Christmas. How would you feel about me asking Jack?'

'Very pleased. The more the merrier.'

'Are you sure? I mean, this first one without...' Tears filled her eyes.

Arthur stroked her cheek. 'Rose, darling, this one's going to be the hardest to bear wherever I am and whoever I'm with. With Jack there, too, I'll have to make even more of an effort and, believe me, it'll be better for all of us that way.'

'Okay, I'll ask him. Now you go back and lose some more of your hard earned savings on the gee-gees. I'll see you on Thursday.'

Arthur watched her go. She was so like a younger version of Evelyn; slim and youthful, graceful but bouncy. But Evelyn had not spent over half of her life in jeans and paint splashed shirts and fishermen's jumpers. She had been brought up in a different era. He smiled as he wondered just how much Rose imagined he spent on betting. It wasn't much, just a couple of pounds a couple of times a week. And it gave him something to do. First he went out to buy the paper then he sat down to pick his horses. That done, he walked down to Newlyn to the tiny, privately owned betting shop belonging to a local family, one of the few such establishments left in the country, he guessed. He was beginning to be recognised by some of the regulars, which was an added bonus.

The last televised race of the day was about to start. Maybe this time he'd picked a winner.

The house was warm when Rose got home. The sun was still shining through the sitting-room window and the heating had switched itself on half an hour previously. While the kettle boiled she cleaned her brushes and stacked her gear in the larder. Jack would be there later, although she had no idea what time or whether he wanted to eat with her. With her stockpile of fish it was never a problem feeding other people. Most of it she had to freeze but it could be cooked without thawing. She was longing to know what had happened to Beth's jacket and why it had not been found.

With a notepad in front of her she began to make a list for her Christmas shopping. She didn't usually bother much, just gifts for her parents and close friends. If she was on her own her meal would be whatever she fancied. Buying cakes and biscuits and chocolates would be wasteful, as she did not enjoy sweet things. This year would be different. She would do the whole thing for the two men who meant the most to her. She had only taken the first sip of her tea when the telephone rang. It was Jack.

'I can make it about six, if that's all right,' he said..

'That's fine. Shall I cook?'

'No. Why don't we go out to eat?'

'It suits me, but it's my turn to pay.' Jack nearly always insisted on paying the bill. It embarrassed Rose, who could pay her way and who always bought her round in the pub. It was a trait she had inherited from her father.

'We'll see. I'll get there as soon as I can.'

Rose hung up. There were many questions she

wanted to ask him but she knew that she would learn nothing over the telephone, especially from the one in Jack's office. She knew from Laura, who had gone to school with Jack and had later met his wife, that he had never discussed his cases with her. What Rose didn't know was whether that was because Marian was indifferent to his work or whether it was a compliment to herself in that Jack trusted her enough to realise that she would never repeat anything he told her. She would have to wait to have her curiosity satisfied. What she had also learnt from Laura was that Jack's divorce was not the usual cliché of busy policeman/ neglected wife. 'It was such a shame, really. They got on so well and they were both good with the boys, it was just that neither of them could settle in the others' territory. Marian was a real city girl, and Jack, well, he'd never be happy anywhere other than Cornwall. Anyway, for your sake I'm glad it happened, even if, at times, you make that man's life a misery.' Rose smiled, recalling Laura's words. The relationship was fine as it was and at least they were both free. David had been dead for almost five years when she met Jack and by that time he had been divorced for ten.

The tea was cold. She made some more and carried on with her list.

Now that she didn't have food to prepare she could spend some time in the attic where paperwork awaited her. She had already decided that all six watercolours for the set of notelets she was working on for Barry would depict subtropical plants. They would form an unusual set. These she could continue to work on through the winter, if the weather allowed, rather than wait, as she usually did, for spring when the wild hedgerow flowers bloomed.

Darkness had fallen by the time she had finished but the attic was bright with spotlights. She decided it was time to shower and change.

Tingling from the heat of the water, Rose put on a cream, boat-neck sweater and a flowing skirt in shades of rust. The tops of her best leather boots were hidden beneath its hem. Her hair, freshly washed, hung softly to her shoulders and she'd made her face up lightly. Casual, but smart, she told her reflection in the cheval mirror which stood in the corner of her bedroom. She folded her jeans and put them on a shelf in the cupboard, which was built in to the wall. Also fitted with a hanging rail, it had become her wardrobe.

She was in the kitchen when Jack tapped on the window, startling her. 'I didn't hear the car.'

'I didn't bring it. It's chilly, but dry so I thought

we'd walk, and that way you don't get to drink more than your share of the wine.' He kissed her. 'You look nice.'

'Thank you.' It was as much of a compliment as she could expect from Jack. 'Where are we going?'

'I've booked a table at the Renaissance.'

'Lovely. Well I'm ready. Shall we go?'

Rose locked up then they walked down the hill, passing the harbour which, because of the suitable weather, was almost denuded of fishing boats, then on past the lighted windows of pubs and cottages. The salvage tug was still there, an oasis of light in the inky water. The clearness of the night meant that the constellations were easily recognisable. It was David who had taught her their various names. Sounds carried across the water in the still air; metal on metal, someone working on a boat, perhaps, and the chug of a trawler out in the bay, its lights just visible as it neared the horizon.

There were no street lights along the path which ran along beside the beach although, on the other side of the main road from which they were divided by the gardens an orange glow could be seen between the palm trees. On a cloudy night it was hard to tell if anyone was walking towards you but at least it meant it remained unspoiled.

Jack was quiet; deep in thought. Rose knew he needed time to unwind, that once they were seated and the wine had been poured he would begin to talk. Or she hoped that he would.

They passed the white walls of the open-air swimming pool, now closed for the winter and for the annual repairs that were always required because of the battering it took from the sea which both surrounded and fed it. They reached Penzance harbour where the Scillonian was being overhauled, along with other large vessels, and came to Ross Bridge. This could be swung open when a ship was coming in to the dry dock. Traffic then had to find an alternative route in and out of the town.

The Renaissance was a restaurant in the Wharfside shopping centre, which by most standards was small. It was built on two levels; the lower one was opposite the harbour. The upper level, above which were luxury flats, was reached by stairs and an escalator or could be approached directly from Market Jew Street which was much higher up. The Renaissance was on the upper level and had marvellous views.

They were lucky, their table was in the window and they could see the harbour and the lights around the bay. Jack ordered a bottle of wine. 'We'd like it straight away, please,' he told the cheerful young waitress.

Rose lit a cigarette and waited, wondering how long it would be before Jack felt like talking. For the moment he was busy alternating his gaze between the menu and the specials board on the wall behind him.

By the time they had ordered Rose's impatience was beginning to show. She fiddled with the crockery, bit her lower lip and avoided making eye contact with Jack. When she finally looked up he was leaning back in his chair, arms folded, a wide smile on his face. 'You deserve a medal,' he said.

'For what?'

'For not asking. Your curiosity, as we all know to our cost, is boundless. I've been expecting to be bombarded with questions ever since I arrived to pick you up. Why the sudden reticence?'

Rose shrugged. 'I can guess what the past week's been like for you. I didn't want to harass you.'

'You do that by merely existing.'

'Well, if you're going to be like that I . . .'

But before she could finish he held up a hand. 'Whoa. That was supposed to be a joke.' He was

248

surprised at her reaction; Rose very rarely lost her sense of humour.

'I'm sorry. I really don't know what's wrong with me. I suppose it's because I can't stop thinking about what happened to Beth.'

'If it makes you feel any better, your information was more than helpful.' He topped up their wine glasses then leant forward with his arms resting on the table. 'I spoke to Sally Jones myself. As Norma Penhalligon stated, Beth was wearing her coat when they left the house. There was no lift, no passing motorist, Sally and Beth walked down to the beach together, and alone. Sally swears that Beth had her coat with her, that when she last saw her she was wearing it. She was still wearing it when we found her, therefore, logically, she had to have had it with her when she was taken.' Jack waited whilst she took this in; he was more than interested in what her response would be.

'No.' Rose shook her head. 'No, Jack, that just isn't so. Beth held up both arms when she asked that man to pick her up. All she had on was jeans, a shirt and a jumper. I swear to you, Jack, she did not have a coat.'

He had been certain that this was what she would say, but in a few seconds, a very few seconds in which she had no idea that anything was amiss, how could she be so certain of what she had seen? On the other hand, hadn't she always been able to describe things with accuracy? Her eye for detail was amazing and he trusted it totally. If she was right then where was the coat between the time of Beth's abduction and when her body was found? He decided to leave it there for the moment, but there was something he wanted to ask Rose to do sometime in the near future.

'What about the boyfriend? Carol's bloke? Did she tell you his name?'

'Yes. He's called Marcus Wright. He's the manager of a shop.' Jack was not about to tell Rose which one because he wouldn't put it past her to go there and find an excuse to talk to him.

'And?'

'It would appear he's innocent, apart from a spot of adultery. We were doubly suspicious when we discovered that he'd taken the week off. It seemed too coincidental that Beth went missing during that time. However, he had hoped to see Carol that day but she'd put him off. Anyway, despite the fact that he wasn't at work he has an alibi for most of Tuesday; at least, for the relevant period. He and a friend were working on his car. We checked, of course. The friend confirmed this, as did several of Wright's neighbours who had seen the two men in his garage. Despite the weather they were working with the door open.

'He was amazed and extremely indignant that we thought he was somehow involved. Anyway, he told me that the affair was over, had, in fact, ended last night.'

'Yes, I know.'

'You know? How?'

Their food arrived. Rose picked up her knife and fork but Jack wanted an answer before he began to eat.

'Geoff Carter told me. He left a message to say that Carol had left him a message – does that make sense? She thanked him and said she had sorted out her problems. I guessed it was that way around. She might be obsessional but she didn't strike me as the sort of person to just give up and walk away from so much, especially when children are involved.'

'But you half suspect her of murder,' Jack stated sardonically.

'You've always said that everyone's a suspect until proved otherwise. And I didn't say I suspected her, I just happened to mention the sibling rivalry and wondered if it was relevant. It was Laura who made me spot it.'

Jack sighed, wondering whether it was worth the Devon and Cornwall police being in existence. Rose, Geoff, Laura and Doreen all seemed to be as much, if not more in the know than they were. Only Barry Rowe and Arthur seemed to be exempt. Unless, of course, there were things Rose wasn't telling him. He would not be surprised if this was the case.

The food arrived; large bowls of homemade soup to start with. 'Let's eat before this gets cold,' Rose said, thus ending the conversation but not the speculation about Bethany Jones. She did not have a coat, Rose was thinking. I know she didn't. And Jack had already decided that he would ask Rose to have a look at the clothes Beth had been wearing that fateful Tuesday.

They walked back briskly because it was much colder than when they had set out. The wind was coming from the east. It blew Rose's hair forwards and into her face. She clasped it and tucked it into the collar of her coat, but it felt good, walking off the meal in the clean, crisp air.

'Want to come in for coffee?' Jack asked when they reached the bottom of Morrab Road, on the corner of which was the Queen's hotel whose large windows faced the sea. When David was alive, on some winter afternoons they would sit inside with a pot of tea or coffee and slices of moist cherry cake. David would read the paper whilst Rose studied the passing pedestrians and any movement in the bay.

'Yes, why not?' It had been some time since she had been to Jack's flat.

They walked up the hill past the dental practice Rose conscientiously attended every six months; towards Morrab Road and Jack's flat. It was a place she had always found comfortable, the large rooms and high ceilings appealing to her artist's eye.

Once inside they went straight to the kitchen where Jack filled and plugged in the kettle. Unlike Rose's, his coffee was instant. He had an early start so he did not want anything more to drink in the way of alcohol.

Now, out of the biting wind and with the heating having been on all evening, Jack felt warm. He took off his jacket and hung it over the back of a chair where it immediately fell to the floor. Wallet, keys, a diary and a photograph fell out.

It was Rose who bent to pick the things up. 'Who's this?' she asked, holding out the picture.

When Jack told her she sank back into her

chair. Her face was white and her hands shook. She prayed she wasn't going to vomit. What she had done was truly terrible.

On that same Monday morning Marcus Wright asked for, and got a transfer to another branch of the shop. There was a vacancy coming up soon in Truro. He didn't mind where it was as long as it wasn't Penzance. A true Cornishman, he did not want to leave the county but now it was time for a change.

No woman had affected him the way in which Carol had done, but it was over, she had made that quite clear and he had no option but to accept it. For the moment he would commute, when the spring came he would put his house on the market and make a totally new start.

He wondered if he would ever get over Carol. He also wondered whether he would ever get over the fact that he had been considered as a murder suspect. All in all, he was better keeping right away from that family.

When Sue Overton collected Katy from school on Monday afternoon her face was pale. Yesterday's trip to Paradise Park had not been the success they had anticipated. Halfway through the afternoon

Katy had reverted to her quiet self and not even the colourful tropical birds she loved could cheer her up again.

On seeing her daughter now, Sue knew the time had come for something to be said. She would mention it, as tactfully as possible, to Simon that night.

'A policeman came to school today,' Katy was saying.

Sue's mouth went dry. Had Katy confided in a teacher instead of herself? 'Oh? What was that for?' She hoped her voice sounded normal.

'To talk to us. He said we must never take sweets or money from strangers, and never, ever to go off with someone we don't know. But I knew that already, Mummy, because you've told me.'

'You never have, have you?' she asked casually, quietly, not wishing to alarm Katy.

'Of course not.' Her indignant tone told Sue she was telling the truth.

The day was beginning to turn colder as the wind changed direction and blew up river, but Katy's hand was warm in hers.

The pattern of the past few weeks was repeated. Katy said she was hungry then left most of her tea. 'Would you like uncle Keith to come and stay again?' The words were out of her mouth before she had time to assess what they might do to Katy. Katy shook her head. 'Don't you like him?' It had been his first visit since Katy's birth because he had been working overseas as a medical volunteer until recently.

'Yes, I do, but he's very noisy.'

It was true. Unlike Simon, Keith was loud and boisterous and seemed to fill any room he was in. Sue decided she could not question Katy further. But why, if she liked him, didn't she want him to come back? Could you like someone who had abused you? Possibly abused you, she amended mentally.

When Katy was in bed and Sue was alone with Simon she made some tea and they sat in the lounge drinking it before she started the evening meal. She finally found the courage to speak the words she had been dreading saying. 'I don't know if you've noticed, but Katy's only been like this since Keith came to stay.'

'No, I hadn't noticed.' He frowned. 'Just what are you implying, Sue?'

'I'm not sure. It's probably coincidence,' she added to soften the blow. She went on to explain Katy's side of the brief conversation they had had concerning her uncle.

Simon was rigid in his armchair. 'If he's so much as touched her in any way, I'll kill the bastard.'

Sue had not expected this reaction; anger, yes, but anger with her for even having suggested such a thing about his brother. 'But how on earth do we find out?' Without contacting the police, they had no idea, and the harm that could do might be irrevocable to everyone concerned if they were wrong. If they asked Keith outright he would be bound to deny it, guilty or not, and to ask Katy was impossible.

'We could phrase it very carefully, ask her if he'd cuddled her a lot, something along those lines,' Simon suggested.

But by the time they had eaten, watched some television and decided it was time for bed they were no nearer knowing what they ought to do.

'What's that maid doing out at this time of night?' Doreen Clarke muttered to herself when she got Rose's answering machine instead of the person she wanted to speak to. It was nine fifteen. Doreen and Cyril always went to bed at ten. 'Can you ring me tomorrow, there's something I want to ask you?' She'll know what's what, that's for sure, Doreen thought as she went to make the final mug of tea of the day. Rose would have kept to her word, she always did, and Doreen was eager to hear the outcome.

Seconds before Rose picked up the photograph, Jack was thinking about what PC Roberts had reported back. Roberts had been the man chosen to attend the school and talk to the children. Rose had told him which one Katy Overton attended so it had not been necessary to go elsewhere. A tactful telephone call to the headmaster had ensured a few minutes were made available in the curriculum. Roberts had delivered his talk and said he would be around for a while if anyone felt the need to speak to him. He had then seen each of the teachers in turn because he had been told not to alert Katy's teacher that they were looking at one particular child. But it was only Katy's teacher who expressed any concern. She confirmed that the girl had become quieter. 'She's fine in the classroom, as bright as ever, and at lunch. But there are times when she's in the playground or not being supervised that she seems, well, not worried, exactly, but forlorn. And there's another thing; she doesn't mix as well as she used to do.'

'Have you spoken to her?' Roberts had enquired.

'Yes, of course, but she insists there's nothing wrong.'

And that was as far as it had gone. However, Jack had taken hope in the fact that Katy's schoolwork wasn't suffering. Deterioration was one of the first signs of abuse. If something was wrong then the child wasn't saying and, according to Rose, her GP had found no cause for alarm. But Doreen Clarke had done so and had therefore confided in Rose knowing that she would pass the information on to himself. And Doreen wouldn't do that without justification. She might be a gossip but she was not an attention seeker or a troublemaker.

And then he had taken off his jacket and hung it carelessly over the back of a chair. It was Rose who bent down to retrieve his bits and pieces. 'Who's this?' she asked.

Jack was puzzled. 'It's Beth. Who did you think it was?' They all had copies of the photograph supplied by Sally Jones, no longer needed now that Beth had been found. Jack had forgotten he still had it. 'Rose, what is it?' She looked ill, her face was white as she slumped back into her chair. 'That's not Beth.' She swallowed. 'I mean, that's not the little girl I saw.'

'Oh, Christ Almighty.' He rarely blasphemed

but the enormity of what Rose had said hit him hard. Surely she had seen the newspapers. But of course, it immediately explained the absence of the coat. Rose's statement was now worthless. What she had seen was probably an innocent father picking up his own child who, naturally, would go with him willingly. This was a major step backwards, not forwards.

'I'm so sorry, Jack. I'm so very sorry.' Tears filled her eyes but she brushed them away, angry with herself for wanting to cry, angrier still for having wasted everyone's time. 'She fitted the description and she must have been about the same age. And, seeing her picture now, they were very similar, the same colour and length of hair.' Stop babbling, she told herself, you've done enough damage already.

So Sally had been telling the truth about the coat. What was odd, though, was that although Rose had believed she had witnessed the crime, no one had witnessed the actual one. Beth Jones had disappeared from that beach without anyone noticing, had been taken willingly, or unwillingly without a single person being aware of it.

CHAPTER TWELVE

Geoff Carter had watched the early morning news on television and knew that, out of common courtesy, he must offer his condolences to Carol Harte. She was, after all, Beth's aunt and the child had now been officially identified. A note did not seem appropriate after she had confided in him so openly and a visit might come across as too personal after what had actually been only a brief acquaintanceship. Never feeling comfortable in such circumstances he decided he would telephone immediately before he lost his nerve.

The phone rang for a long time. He was about to hang up when she answered.

'Hello.' The word was softly spoken yet it expressed the depth of her grief and exhaustion. In the background were children's voices.

'Carol, it's Geoff Carter. I don't want to intrude and I really don't know what to say except how very, very sorry I am.'

'Oh, Geoff.' Her next words were muffled by sobs.

'Look, are you on your own, Carol?'

'No; the children are here. I picked them up on Sunday but I haven't let them go to school this week. I've explained what's happened but I'm not sure they fully understand.'

Geoff thought it would be better if she had an adult with her. Tuesday was a quiet day, he could close the gallery and go himself. But two things suggested that this was not a good idea. She might mistake his intentions or the children might say something to their father about his visit and cause further complications. There was also the chance that he might lose business. You coward, he thought as a more logical idea occurred to him. 'Why don't I ring Rose Trevelyan and ask her to come and sit with you for a while.' Rose would probably curse him for suggesting it but he felt he had to do something.

'Yes. Would you? Right now I really wish that John was here.'

Geoff was not sure whether John was the husband or the abandoned lover so made no comment. 'I'll speak to her right away. If she doesn't get back to you within a few minutes then you'll know she's not in, but I'll keep trying.'

Rose was at home but her manner was a little brusque when she answered the phone. She listened to Geoff's proposal, unsure how she felt about it. But it was her innate kindness that prompted her answer. 'Yes, I'll go over there right away. Does she need food or anything for the children?'

'I didn't think to ask, actually. Do let me know how it goes.'

Guilt, she thought, as she got ready to go out. He's being solicitous but he doesn't want to go himself. She rang Carol to say she was on her way.

The car needed petrol. Rose filled the tank at the Co-op then drove to Marazion. There, she bought some chocolate for the children.

Carol opened the door as soon as she heard the engine of the car. Behind her were two small girls, their eyes wide with curiosity. Carol's hair was unkempt and there was a stain on her blouse but it was her face that startled Rose more. Carol seemed to have aged by about ten years and her eyes were red-rimmed with crying. 'Come in, and thank you so much for coming. I just didn't know who to turn to. Sally only wants Mum with her.' Mum should be with me, she was thinking. I'm the one who needs her now.

Although Carol and Sally did not get on, Rose realised that Carol had loved her niece. Beth, she now saw, looked very much like her cousins. 'Hello, my name's Rose,' she said to the solemn-faced girls. Carol introduced them as Tamsin and Lucy. 'Are they allowed chocolate?' Rose whispered. Their mother nodded.

'Thank you,' they said in turn as they were handed a small bar each.

'Why don't you play in one of your bedrooms,' Carol suggested as she sat down and indicated for Rose to do the same. They disappeared obediently, unsure as to what was going on, what had happened to their mother and who the stranger was who had brought them chocolate.

'Shall I make you some coffee?'

Carol looked at Rose with a vacant expression as if she had forgotten why she was there. Suddenly tears filled her eyes. 'I'm sorry, I'm not used to people being nice to me.'

'I won't be long.' Rose got up. She thought

the self-pity was a bit over the top. Had Carol no idea how her sister must be feeling?

That Carol was grieving was evident. The kitchen was not exactly a mess but it was far from its previous immaculate state.

Rose felt awkward rummaging around in someone else's cupboards but Carol looked in need of sustenance. And what about Tamsin and Lucy? Had they been fed? Were they thirsty? A bar of chocolate was hardly a balanced meal.

Having found all that she required she went into the hall. Sounds could be heard from behind a closed door. She knocked quietly then opened it. 'Are you two hungry?'

'Have you got some more chocolate?' This was from Tamsin who, at six, was not about to miss a chance of a bit of exploitation.

'No, there's no more. Have you had breakfast?'

It was Lucy who spoke. 'Yes. Tamsin did us some cereals and made toast in the toaster but she got in a mess with the butter and jam. We're not allowed to use the grill.'

'Okay. Would you like a drink then?'

Both girls nodded. Rose had noticed a carton of orange juice in the fridge. She went to pour some wondering what they would have for lunch and if she should offer to stay and make it.

Carol was blowing her nose when Rose carried in the coffee tray. Unlike her own bright ceramic mugs with their hand painted tulips, Carol's were bone china, white, with a thin gold rim, part of a complete dinner service that was stacked in the cupboard. Rose hoped the girls would not spill their orange juice on the white bedroom carpet. Madness, Rose thought. Who would choose to lay such a colour in a child's bedroom?

Carol's hands shook as she picked up her mug. With a sodden tissue she wiped her eyes again. 'I loved Beth so very much. I don't think I'll ever get over this.'

Rose, whose tolerance was usually endless, except where Jack was concerned, found her patience wearing thin. 'But just imagine how Sally must feel,' she said as calmly as possible. 'She is, after all, Beth's mother.'

'No. No, she isn't.' Carol jerked upright spilling coffee over the arm of the chair. 'I'm Beth's mother.' The outburst seemed to have left her shocked and drained. She slumped back into the seat, her hand to her mouth, aghast at what she had just said.

Rose was too shocked to speak. Could it be true or was this another aspect of Carol's insecurity, because surely her obsessional traits were proof of insecurity. 'What do you mean?' she finally managed to ask.

Those four words had opened the floodgates. Rose listened with incredulity until she recognised the ring of truth. Almost five years of bottled up emotion and guilt came pouring out for had she not abandoned the child she would still be alive. Her guilt must be equal to, if not more than, Sally's.

No wonder she's like she is, Rose thought. What a terrible strain to have endured for so long, and now it had ended in tragedy.

The morning had passed but Rose knew she could not simply leave. She had to ensure Carol would not do something stupid and that, after her confession, she was still capable of looking after her two small daughters, daughters who had been very quiet for a long time. She hoped they were behaving themselves rather than taking advantage of the strange situation. Maybe, after lunch, she might manage half a day's work. The weather wasn't great but at least it wasn't raining. 'I'll feed the children and make you a sandwich,' she said, desperate for a few minutes alone to think things over.

'Can you cook sausages?' Tamsin asked suspiciously when Rose offered to get them something to eat. 'Because that's what we'd like, isn't it, Lucy?' Lucy nodded. 'And beans.'

'What, no chips?' Rose smiled when their eyes lit up.

'Oh, yes, please. Mum gets the frozen ones from Iceland. Shall I show you where we keep them?'

Rose had spotted the freezer but she dutifully followed the children to the kitchen where they took pride in finding the things she needed. They then sat at the kitchen table watching with awe as Rose oven baked and grilled and stirred beans in the pan.

Whilst they were eating, the chips smothered with an amount of tomato sauce she was sure was more than they were normally permitted, she made a cheese salad sandwich and took it in to Carol who sat with her eyes closed.

Thank you, Rose, you're very kind. I do appreciate what you've done for us,' she said as she took the plate. 'There's one thing, you won't repeat what I've told you, will you? I mean to my sister. Naturally she knows the story, apart from who the actual father is.' Already she was regretting the outburst and seemed to be embarrassed by it, but it was too late to alter the fact it had taken place.

Rose didn't know how to reply. Was the information relevant to Beth's murder? It didn't seem likely but if it was the case she would have to tell Jack. 'I promise I won't say a word to your family but it might be necessary to mention it to the police.'

'Why? Why would the police want to speak to you?' Panic showed in her face.

'Because I was a witness.' Or thought I was, and because I know the officer in charge of the case and he knows me, she added silently. Once Jack learnt she had been at Carol's place, and he would do, he always discovered her movements, he would demand to know what they had talked about and she would have to tell him.

'Of course, I'm sorry. I forgot.'

Rose just stopped herself from revealing the truth, that it was not Beth she had seen but an innocent man with a girl who was presumably his daughter, but that would have made matters even worse. No longer being a genuine witness would lessen the leverage she had with the women involved.

Carol managed to eat her sandwich and drink the coffee that came with it. Satisfied that she would be able to cope, Rose decided it was time to leave.

'On reflection, I'm glad someone finally knows the truth,' she said as she showed Rose to the door. 'And thank you again for all you've done.'

'We'll look after Mummy,' Tamsin assured her as she and Lucy heard sounds of departure and came to investigate. 'Daddy says we have to when he's away. He's coming home tomorrow. Mummy phoned him, because of Beth. She's in heaven with Jesus now.'

So Carol had explained as best she was able and in a way which made sense to her children. 'I'm glad, and I'm sure you'll be pleased to see him.'

'Yes, we will. He usually brings us a present,' Lucy commented hopefully.

Rose tried not to smile at the avarice of the child but doubted he would think of doing so under the circumstances. She left the three of them standing in the doorway and sensed they would pull through eventually, especially as John was now on his way home.

Sally Jones needed to be alone. She had been through so much during the course of a week and the flat seemed to have been full of people ever since last Tuesday 'Go back home, Mum, I'll be fine, honestly. And think of the business.

With Christmas coming up you'll lose trade.' She wished she hadn't mentioned Christmas. 'I promise I'll let you know as soon as we can fix a date for the funeral.' That would be another milestone to get over; it would, she supposed, also be the final hurdle. She would first have to attend the inquest.

Alice, too, would be pleased to go home. Of course she had come when her daughter needed her but she was wise enough to realise that there were limits to being in close confinement with people you love. Now they both needed time to adjust, to face their grief in their individual ways. She would drive back first thing in the morning.

It was odd that neither of them mentioned Carol although they knew the reason she had only made contact once since hearing the news. Alice knew it would have been kind to see her before she left but she made do with a telephone call, wondering at her inability to love her younger child.

Michael Poole was devastated. At first, numb with shock and disbelief, he doubted he would ever feel anything again. Hours later, alone in his room, the pain had registered and he had cried. His sadness was as much for what he had missed and what might have been as much as it had been for what had happened to Beth.

Detective Inspector Pearce had, at some point, explained that the post mortem showed that Beth had been smothered but that it was highly unlikely she had known what was happening to her. Before that he had asked him if he took sleeping pills.

'No,' he had said, believing at the time that he was about to be offered the services of a local doctor if he felt the need for them.

'Does Sally?'

'Not to my knowledge. At least, she didn't when we lived together. Why do you want to know?'

'Because traces of barbiturate were found in Beth's blood sample. She was probably unconscious at the time of her death.'

It was some comfort but Michael realised that the question meant they were all still suspects.

That had been on the Sunday evening. On Tuesday morning, feeling a little stronger, he had gone to see Sally but she was too distraught to speak to him. Michael decided he might as well return to work. Alice would let him know when the funeral was to take place but he understood that it might not be for some time. The date would depend upon when, or if, they found Beth's murderer.

He looked at his watch. It was eleven fifteen. He might just as well leave now. There would be things to attend to at home after a week's absence.

Downstairs he asked the hotelier for his bill then used the payphone in the hall. His mobile battery was flat and he hadn't brought the charger because he had imagined only staying a day or so.

'I'll be back tomorrow,' he told his boss, the words of condolence barely registering. What he really wanted to do was to find the murdering bastard who'd robbed him of a daughter and slowly torture him, but what chance did he have when the police didn't seem to be getting anywhere?

He disconnected the line and found more change then rang the Camborne number and asked to be put through to Inspector Pearce. 'It's Michael Poole. I just wanted to check that it's all right for me to go back to Looe.'

'Yes, that's fine, but we need to know where you are in case there are any developments, so if you intend going anywhere, would you let us know?'

'Of course.' Any developments. He knew what

that meant. They still suspected him even though his alibi was watertight. Why? Because, he assumed, alibis could be arranged, or fixed, or whatever the jargon was.

He packed his small bag, paid his bill and left. He never wanted to see Marazion again.

In typical West Cornwall fashion the weather changed and clouds began to gather. Within minutes the sky was a pearly grey and the first spots of rain began to fall. Rose sighed. So much for her plans for the afternoon. She had intended continuing working on the mine scene which was already pleasing to the eye. It was exactly the sort of oil that sold well in Geoff's gallery. For some reason she felt in need of company other than her own. She went outside and got back into the car again.

When she reached Penzance she parked, pulled her raincoat from the back seat of the car and walked down the hill to Barry's shop. Like the man himself, this, too, had received a facelift but that was due to Daphne Hill rather than its owner. Daphne had taken it upon herself to rearrange the stock, thus making more room for browsers, and whilst she was doing so she had cleaned all the shelves.

Barry was spending more time at the print

works in Camborne where he oversaw the production of his specialised greetings cards and other stationery. He also spent time with Jenny. Rose was in luck, Barry was at the back of the shop making a stock list when she arrived.

'Hello Daphne, how's things?'

'Fine, thanks, Rose. You?'

'Could be better. I was hoping to work.' She looked towards the window where raindrops glistened. 'Is Barry around?'

'I am.' He appeared in the doorway. 'I heard your voice. How are you, stranger?'

'I saw you on Sunday, it's only Tuesday.' She smiled at his absentmindedness.

Wrong move, he thought, I shouldn't have mentioned Sunday. And Rose, despite the smile, looked worried. 'I think this can wait.' He put the folder he was holding beneath the counter. 'Fancy a coffee or a drink?'

'It's early, even by my standards, but I could do with the latter. Let me get the car then I can drive us down to the Yacht. I can pick it up tomorrow.'

'I'll come with you. Will you be all right, Daphne?'

'Of course I'll be all right. You're such a worrier, Barry.' But she softened her words with a kind smile. 'Do you want me to lock up?'

Barry looked startled. 'It's only half-past two, we're not going to be that long.'

Daphne grinned at Rose. 'It would do him good to let his hair down once in a while.'

'Oh, I think he's getting there even if it has taken him several decades.' Rose liked Daphne who was a sensible, hardworking, down-to-earth woman who had been through a bad time and survived it. She was solidly built and took pride in her appearance – even if she wore more makeup and the costume jewellery than was necessary. She and her husband, Rod, had moved to Cornwall to escape their troubles and had settled in quickly, unlike many who missed the facilities of the towns and cities outside the county. Progress was being made, whether for good or bad, and some of the Penzance shops now stocked things unheard of five years ago in the way of food, but few newcomers appreciated that life was very much slower, that queues formed in shops because conversations took priority over speed. Even Rose, more accepting than the likes of Doreen and Cyril Clarke, was sorry that housing was becoming unaffordable for locals because prices were rocketing and so very many people were on the minimum wage. Let them come, she thought, but let them accept how it is here and not try to bring all they believed they wanted to leave behind with them.

Rose and Barry hurried to the car. The wind was blowing harder, heavier rain would follow. Rose drove the short distance to the seafront where there was unlimited parking. If the wind kept up the car would be grimed with salt by the time she collected it.

The Yacht Inn, like the open air Jubilee Pool opposite, was of art deco design and had been built in the 1930s. The bar area was spacious with a large bay window on the lower level and smaller ones on the upper, through all of which the panorama of the bay could be seen. A rolling swell was surging in on the tide. It looked harmless, unlike the breakers which often smashed against the Promenade wall, but it was this motion which caused the most seasickness.

The usual early afternoon crowd were seated on the high stools at the bar; the landlord of another local pub which shut at half-past two on winter afternoons, a retired garage owner from Buryas Bridge, a court bailiff and an ex-CID officer who had retired through injury. Rose knew and liked them all. She turned and waved to a sprightly and dapper nonagenarian who came in every day for lunch and went home by taxi.

'Now, what's on your mind?' Barry asked once he had ordered their drinks and paid the young barman who, he knew, played for the local rugby club.

'That's the problem, I can't tell you. I'm sorry, Barry, it's something that was told to me in confidence.'

'Fair enough.' There was no point in pursuing it, Rose would never break her word. 'But I can take it it's to do with Beth.'

'Yes, unfortunately it is. And I honestly don't know what to do about it.'

'What you mean is, should you tell Jack.' He was grinning. At times like this he could read her like a book but mostly she remained enigmatic. Rose Trevelyan, he thought, was a very complex creature and at that moment looked lovely with her hair wavier from the rain and her raincoat making her seem more petite than she actually was. He caught a glimpse of himself in the mirror which lined the wall behind the bar and stood straighter. He had always been drop-shouldered and he couldn't help the fact that his hair was thinning and he had to wear glasses but he was glad that, at Rose's insistence, he had finally invested in a whole wardrobe of new clothes.

'You've got it in one.'

'Then tell him; at least it'll be off your conscience if it's relevant to the case.' He was ashamed to admit that he enjoyed seeing her get one over on Jack. As much as he liked and admired the man he had been the cause of much jealousy over the last four or five years. At least Rose had not given in and agreed to live with him. Barry was aware that what he felt for Jenny had not lessened his feelings for Rose but he was now wise enough to realise that he couldn't go on chasing that dream for ever.

'Maybe I will.' In fact, I know I'll have to, she thought reluctantly. It was a peculiar situation although she had heard of instances where a grandmother had passed off her daughter's illegitimate child as her own. It was not unremarkable when women became grandmothers in their thirties.

Carol loved and wanted her child but to have kept her would have finished her marriage. Sally, having brought Beth up since she was a tiny baby, probably hadn't wanted to share her. This could explain the antipathy between the sisters and the reason why Alice Jones favoured Sally. It must have been hard for her to watch one of them produce a child she couldn't keep whilst the other longed for a baby of her own. Yet

Carol had risked her marriage a second time by having an affair with Marcus. Accepted, that was over now, but she had still taken the risk. She's lonely, Rose guessed, lonely and guilty and has no one in whom to confide. Maybe she wanted to get caught, maybe it would be some sort of punishment to show how unworthy she was.

'Hello?' Barry tapped her gently on the head. 'What?'

'You were miles away. I asked if you fancied sharing a curry with me tonight.'

'No, not tonight, thanks, Barry. Later in the week, if you like. Aren't you seeing Jenny?'

He shook his head. 'She's at her Italian class.' Neither of them had any idea why she went because she disliked foreign travel. But Jenny took a different adult education course every year. 'At least let me buy you another drink.'

It showed how worried she was when Rose didn't insist it was her round.

Rose knew she was being antisocial, too preoccupied in her own thoughts, so she made an effort at conversation and mentioned the notelets she was currently working on.

'Excellent idea. When will they be ready?'

'In a week or so, weather depending, of course.'

Barry left after the second drink. He was no daytime drinker and he didn't want to fall asleep in front of one of his favourite television programmes later that night.

'Lightweight,' Rose teased as he kissed her goodbye. 'I'll stay a bit longer and chat to the usual suspects.'

It was after four by the time she started to walk home. She was glad that she had stayed; the conversation had been stimulating and had taken her mind off Beth for a while.

The wind had dropped and the rain had eased but everything was shrouded in drizzle. All was now still and damp. Rose was thankful for her raincoat but soon warmed up as she walked briskly towards home. She had had to leave the car but she cursed when the Mousehole bus – which stopped wherever passengers requested it to and would have taken her to the bottom of her drive – passed her between stops without her having seen it coming.

As soon as she got indoors she rang Jack. He wasn't in his office at Camborne and he didn't answer his mobile so she left a message. Within half an hour he rang back. 'You said to call you, what's the matter now?'

'Don't snap at me, Jack.'

'I didn't mean to. I apologise.'

Rose heard the tension in his voice and realised how much pressure he would be under to solve the case. 'I was ringing to see if you'd like to come over later. I'll cook you a meal.'

'That would be lovely. I think I can get away by seven. And, Rose, I really am sorry for snapping.'

There was time to make a bit of an effort. She sipped black coffee and listened to Radio 4 as she stuffed two large mackerel. There was no point in waiting for the local news on Radio Cornwall, Jack would have said if there had been any kind of breakthrough.

Once the vegetables were prepared she showered and changed into clean jeans and a pale green sweater. She didn't bother with makeup but returned to the bedroom to spray on some perfume.

Jack arrived a little after seven, bearing flowers and wine. 'To make up for my teasiness,' he said, smiling at her surprised expression. Wine, yes, but he was not a man to bring flowers. 'And, of course, for suspecting you of meddling.'

Oh, dear, she thought, what's he going to say when I tell him. 'I'll have you know I don't meddle. People simply choose to tell me things.' She had nearly come out with it straight away.

'Are you going to open the wine or shall we just look at it?'

'Why are your cheeks so pink? Have you been on it already?'

'I've just had a shower. But, yes, I did happen to call in to the Yacht on my way home.'

'Ah, that's why there's no car in the drive. Say no more, it'll be our secret.'

Rose didn't know whether she was amused or infuriated, but Jack always had that effect on her. 'The food won't be long. Let's drink this in the sitting-room, I've lit the fire to cheer the place up.'

Jack thought it was unnecessary. Rose's sitting-room was one of the most cheerful rooms he knew of. Outside there was the view of the bay and the busy harbour, inside was her comfortable furniture, her bookcases and the small lamps which lit the room with a cosy glow. He sat down. Add to that the crackling of logs on the fire, the flickering shadows of the flames, a glass of wine and a meal to look forward to; and Rose. What more could a man ask for? One thing: the Beth Jones case to be solved.

'We're having to start all over again. Thinking that Beth went off willingly had us concentrating on her nearest and dearest. But now it's back to square one, it could be anyone.'

All my fault, Rose thought. It's entirely my fault for misleading them but I really thought I was being helpful. Would Beth's life have been saved if I hadn't told them what I thought I had seen? No, probably not, she decided. Jack had said that she had been killed on the Tuesday, the same day as she had been snatched. Whoever had done it could be anywhere in the world by now.

'On the other hand,' Jack continued, 'it may well have been premeditated.'

'How come?'

He told her about the barbiturates. 'Of course, who's to say her abductor didn't always carry them or had just had a prescription filled. We've checked all the local chemists, both here and the one in Marazion. They all know their regular customers and neither Sally nor Carol take them. Poole doesn't either.'

'Could they have got them from someone else? Alice, say, or even Norma Penhalligon.'

'Clever girl. But we've checked that, too. However, the motive still remains unclear. Beth wasn't sexually abused, nor was she hurt in any other way and to drug her first meant that whoever killed her didn't want her to feel anything. It's all so damn confusing, Rose.'

'It still sounds like someone who knew her to

me.' Right, he has to know, and he has to know now. 'I went to see Carol today. And before you say anything, Geoff Carter had rung her and volunteered my services because he told me she was in such a state.'

'And was she in a state?'

'Definitely. And her children were more or less fending for themselves.'

'Well, she's just lost her niece, it's understandable.'

'I don't think you fully understand, Jack.' She took a sip of her wine.

'What, exactly, are you getting at?'

'Carol told me that Beth was her daughter.'

'What?' With the glass halfway to his mouth he almost spilt his drink.

'That's what she told me. And there's definitely a resemblance. It would also explain why she's taking it so badly.'

'Okay, Rose, let's have the whole story.'

Continuing would probably bring trouble to one or both sisters but she had no choice. 'Before Carol met and married John Harte she was going out with Michael Poole. It seems things didn't work out but they weren't helped by the fact that Sally made a play for, and got, Michael. This, apparently, was the pattern of their younger lives. However, Sally and Michael were together for quite a long time and he didn't want the relationship to end. It was Sally who broke it off.

'I know this is going to sound unbelievable, but it rang true to me. Carol already had the two girls but she became pregnant whilst John was working abroad. She was in her third month when he returned. She couldn't bring herself to tell him because he'd know it wasn't his baby. By then it was too late for an abortion. You see, she hadn't realised until it was too late that she was pregnant. Her cycle has never been regular. She had two choices. John wasn't due back again for another six months. She could risk having the baby and try passing it off as his, a baby born prematurely, or she could ask someone else to bring it up for her. Obviously, without John's permission, there was no question of adoption.'

'Are you telling me that Sally broke off her relationship with Poole in order to bring up her sister's child?'

'Yes. As incredible as it seems, that's what she did. But she had ulterior motives. Despite what she told people, Sally was desperate for a child of her own. She gave up her job, moved down here and waited for the baby to be born.'

Jack drained his glass and placed it on the floor

beside his chair. His deep blue eyes registered bewilderment. 'This doesn't pan out. What about the follow up care, the clinics and things that babies are supposed to attend? And there's the financial question. How did she cope?'

'Sally said she never claimed any benefits.'

'So how does she live?' Not solely upon what Poole contributed, he thought.

'It's quite simple: Michael Poole sends money via Alice Jones and Carol gives her the rest. Carol can claim family allowance because she registered the birth legally when she was at her mother's, but she has to be careful where she keeps the book.'

'What's going to happen now? Carol will have to inform the authorities.'

Rose shrugged. 'We didn't go into that much detail. Anyway, to answer your other question, the follow-up care bit was easy. Carol usually took Beth, sometimes Sally did. There would be nothing unusual in one sister helping another out. Once they're not babies fewer and fewer visits are necessary.'

'All right, so far so good, but what about Tamsin and Lucy, surely . . . no, I've got it, they'd have been two and less than one year old respectively then, far too young to realise what was happening. What about friends and neighbours? Surely someone spotted she was pregnant?'

'She says not. She said she kept it hidden for quite a while. And besides, you've been there, there aren't any neighbours. Towards the end Sally moved in and did all her shopping and took the children out. Carol went up to her mother's to have the baby. Meanwhile, Sally found a flat. As soon as Beth was born she moved in with her and everyone assumed it was her child.'

'It seems she went to a good deal of trouble for Carol. And why, then, is Poole paying towards Beth's keep? Did Sally tell him it was his child?'

'Yes. That's why she couldn't see him and didn't want him to find her. He would have known she wasn't pregnant.' Rose smiled. 'But haven't you guessed, Jack? Sally wasn't lying. Beth is his child.'

'Jesus,' he said. The single word was followed by several seconds of silence.

'It was the usual story. Michael had come down from Looe to deliver a piece of furniture Alice was storing for Carol. John was away, as I said, and things developed from there. Michael was only here for one night, Carol swears it was just the once, but she was still breastfeeding Lucy and women are more vulnerable then. At the time

Michael was living with Sally and neither he nor Carol realised the possible consequences.'

'Two more questions. Does Poole know that Beth isn't Sally's child? And does Sally know that Poole is the father?'

'The answer to both is no. Obviously Sally would have refused to take responsibility if she had been aware she had been deceived by both her sister and her boyfriend. Don't forget if Beth really was his child he'd have had to have paid for her keep either way.'

'Um, I wonder.'

But Rose didn't stay to hear what was on his mind. She could smell the fish and went to make sure it was not overcooked. 'It's ready,' she called.

Jack sat at the table and poured more wine as Rose dished up. If Poole had discovered he had been deceived would he have harmed the child? Surely it was more likely he would have wanted revenge on one or both women. But then, killing Beth would have achieved just that. And if Sally had discovered Beth's true parentage, would she have killed her, the child she had cared for for over four years? 'Rose, you're a woman, can you think of any other reason why Sally would have put herself out so greatly?'

'Oh, I thought I'd said. You know now that

Sally had always longed for a child but she was born with an abnormality which made this impossible.'

'And Carol knew this.'

'She did.'

That explained a lot. No wonder she had not hesitated in asking. It also explained Sally's willingness in the matter. But it didn't explain Beth's death.

Rose placed a plate in front of him. Jack picked up his knife and fork. Pungent steam rose from the mackerel which contained an apricot and walnut stuffing; his favourite. It was time to eat and forget work. He would think about all that he had been told in the morning.

Jack helped with the washing up; living alone Rose saw no point in having a dishwasher. They listened to some jazz then, to Rose's surprise, Jack said he was leaving. This was so typical of the way things were with them, their moods were rarely attuned. She had felt in need of the comfort of his body in her bed but she would not admit it and would therefore have to do without it.

'It was, as always, a lovely meal. Thank you, Rose.' He picked up his jacket and gave her a brotherly kiss on the forehead.

So much for passion, Rose thought. She was

disappointed but understood that his mind was on what she had told him. 'Oh, bugger it,' she said as she rinsed out their coffee cups. There was an inch or so of wine left in the bottle, she would drink it by the dying embers of the fire then go to bed and read.

The last log settled sending lively sparks up the chimney. The scent of applewood made her nostalgic. It reminded her of her teenage years, just before she went to college. Her parents had lost an orchard to disease but the wood had not been wasted. How young Arthur and Evelyn had been then, although to her they had not seemed so. And now her mother was dead and her father was living in Penzance. There was no way in which she could have envisaged any of it, her life or that of her parents, when she had been seventeen.

As she cleaned her teeth she realised she had had no contact with Sally since she had heard the news of Beth's death. Should she phone or write or go in person? I'll go, she decided, as she got undressed. When David had died only her true friends had forced themselves upon her, insisting that she ate and slept and didn't drown her sorrows in wine, even though she'd hated what seemed like their interference at the time.

But many people had avoided her initially, out of embarrassment or a fear of making matters worse. It was daft when matters could not have been worse.

Rose took one last, ritualistic look at the bay then drew the curtains. It had been a long day and she was too tired to read. She lay listening to the wind in the chimney breast, the occasional, late screech of a gull and the ticking as the central heating pipes cooled down. Within minutes she had fallen asleep.

CHAPTER THIRTEEN

Carol Harte was not expecting another visit from the police. There was nothing more she could tell them. When she opened the door her stomach turned over. The children were back at school; it was pointless to protect them from what they would have to face eventually, but for a second she thought something had happened to one of them. John would be home that evening. Never had she looked forward to seeing him so much.

Jack had interviewed Carol once but even after that brief acquaintanceship he was shocked at her appearance. Only now, after what Rose had divulged, did he understand the reason for it. At his side was a female detective. 'May we come in?' he asked.

'Yes, of course, I'm sorry.'

They stepped in out of the rain which was sweeping across the countryside. Water dripped from the trees and the shiny leaves of the shrubs glistened wetly. The lowing of a single cow drifted over the fields.

'Would you like some coffee?' Carol asked when she had shown them into the lounge.

'No thank you.' Jack wondered how many times a police officer was asked that question during the course of his or her career.

Carol sat down but did not invite them to do so. 'This is about Beth, I take it.' She gazed at Jack, the pain evident in her face. 'Well, obviously it is.' She paused. 'You know, don't you?'

'Know what, Mrs Harte?'

'That Beth's . . . that she was my daughter.' What else could have brought them? Rose Trevelyan must have told them because surely neither Sally nor her mother would have spoken out after all this time. Thank goodness John was not back yet. Maybe the truth could still be hidden from him. 'Did you kill her, Carol?'

'No. I did not.' She had no real alibi and it probably seemed suspicious that the children were staying with John's mother when Beth had disappeared. They had already asked where she was on that Tuesday but doing housework and shopping was not much of an answer. And who would recall seeing her on that afternoon which was now more than a week ago? She was stunned. How could they imagine she had harmed Beth? 'I didn't kill her but I blame myself. If I'd faced the music at the time and kept Beth she would have been with me and not with Sally.' Her hands were clasped tightly around her knees.

Jack knew that platitudes were a waste of time. Her decision then could not alter what had happened now. 'Will you tell your husband?'

Carol shook her head but it was not a denial. She had no idea if she had the nerve. But he might find out anyway and the truth would be better coming from her rather than another source.

There was not much else Jack could do or say but he decided to question her about her alibi again.

'Wait,' she interrupted him. 'I've just remembered something.' She got up and left the room and returned within minutes carrying a folder. 'My bank bits and pieces. I've got the receipts from my shopping. I always keep them to check against my bank statements.' She shuffled through the slips and handed two to Jack. On the afternoon in question Carol had made purchases with her Switch card. She had bought petrol at two fifty-six at Safeway's filling station and had then gone across the road to the store. There was a long list of goods, it would have taken her some time to fill her trolley, pay and pack it all up. That receipt was timed at three forty-one. It would have been impossible for her to have been on that beach. He asked to see her Switch card. The first numbers, the ones shown on the slip, matched the card. This was hardly a breakthrough but it was one less suspect on the list.

He thanked her for her time and left. The female detective who had remained silent, followed him. 'What worries me, Mandy,' he said to her as they got into the car, 'is that there is still a chance this might have been random. Take that little girl in Hayle, the one who was dragged into a car. There have been no other instances of abuse, no cases even vaguely similar. That was random, I'm sure of it. If the person was a stranger to the area we'll probably never find him.'

Jack started the engine. The rain showed no sign of abating. He flicked on the wiper switch and pressed the one for the demister, then they set off back to Camborne.

'But you don't think Beth's murder was random, do you, sir?'

'No, I don't. The sleeping tablets make me think it was planned.'

'But there doesn't seem to be a motive. Who could possibly gain by her death?'

'Ah, but there always is a motive, no matter how odd it might seem to us.'

They drove on in silence. The tyres hissed on the wet roads and sent spray sideways. On either side, the gently sloping hills with their scattered boulders were shrouded in rain.

'Certainly no one gains financially,' Jack continued once he'd overtaken a slowly moving tractor drawing a trailer full of manure. And then he recalled that Michael Poole had declared Sally Jones to be an unfit mother. How would he know when, supposedly, at the time, he had no contact with either Sally or Beth? That needed a little more looking into. He would, of course, ask.

Apart from the awful weather it was Rose's conscience which dictated that she paid Sally Jones a visit. She watched the rain snaking down the kitchen windows, beyond which a small rivulet ran down the drive. This did not deter a male blackbird whose bright yellow beak was tugging at a worm in the lawn.

Rose finished her coffee, pulled on her raincoat

and went out to the car. When she reached Marazion she parked as near to the house as she was able but was still wet when she reached it. Her hair hung damply and the hems of her jeans were soaked.

She rang the bell. There was no sign of Norma and no lights shone through the downstairs windows. On such a dull day they would have been necessary if anyone was at home.

'Who is it?' a subdued voice enquired metallically through the entry phone system.

'It's Rose Trevelyan.'

The door buzzed. Rose pushed it and went inside. Her feet left wet marks on the spotless black and white tiles but as there was no mat there was little she could do about it.

Sally was waiting at the top of the stairs. She looked even thinner than when Rose had last seen her and she smelt faintly of sweat and quite strongly of alcohol. It was ten fifteen in the morning. But to Rose, both were understandable. She had been through the same when David died. 'Are you up to visitors?'

Sally nodded and led the way into her flat. 'Do you want some coffee, or a drink?' She indicated the cider bottle on the floor beside her chair.

'Coffee, please,' she said, hoping that Sally would join her.

Sally stumbled to the kitchen, swearing as she knocked something over.

She's alone, and she shouldn't be, not yet, Rose decided as she took in her surroundings. But the two sisters would not want to be together and, presumably, Alice Jones had had to go back to look after her business. Norma, she was certain, would have been keeping an eye on her.

Sally returned with the coffee. Rose was about to take a sip when the smell told her that the milk was off. She placed the mug on the floor as there was nowhere else to put it.

Meanwhile, Sally had refilled her glass with cider. 'So you think you saw who took Beth, do you?'

Rose was surprised by the aggression, both in her face and voice, but Jack had warned her not to let on about her mistake. 'It'll make the culprit more confident if he thinks we believe you, and therefore it's more likely he or she will make a mistake,' he had said.

Rose nodded. She could not voice the lie for she had been totally mistaken.

Unexpectedly, Sally laughed. 'Well, it wasn't much help to the police.'

'I'm sorry, Sally. I know how very hard this must be for you.'

'Do you? Do you really? Well you don't know the half of it.' She swallowed more cider and wiped her mouth on the sleeve of her sweatshirt. 'The bastard, how could he do that to me? And her. I might've guessed. It's always been the same. Anything I've ever wanted, she's taken away from me. And then to give me his child to care for, the child that should have been mine, how could she have been so cruel?' She inhaled deeply. 'Bitch,' she shrieked, as if she meant Rose.

Rose held her breath. This meant that Sally had discovered who Beth's father was. But had she only found out recently? If so, who had told her, and why? And if this was the case had she taken it into her head to punish both of Beth's natural parents in one go? Why hadn't she thought of that before? It seemed the obvious solution. And how much harder the news would have hit a woman who was unable to have children whilst her sister had produced a third one she did not want, and that child being the daughter of her own lover.

'Who's a bastard?' Rose asked quietly. She needed to be one hundred per cent certain she'd got things right.

'Michael. Who else would I mean? And that whore of a sister of mine. He said he wanted me back, baby and all, but it was Beth he wanted, I can see that now.'

'But he thought she was yours.'

Sally wasn't listening. 'An unfit mother, that's what he called me. Who does he think he is? He's hardly a paragon of virtue, is he, the shit. My whole life's always been the same; I've always been the loser. Well, I'll show them.' She got up and lurched across the room and out into the hall. Rose heard her fumbling in a drawer and then there was silence.

Another minute passed. Rose got up and went to investigate. The silence had become sinister.

Sally was standing beside the sink, tears rolling down her face. There was a knife in her hand.

'God, no. Wait,' Rose shouted as she ran towards her.

'Get away. I'll kill you first if you try to stop me.'

Frightened that she might just do that, Rose stood still. 'Sally, don't,' she whispered.

'It was Carol who told me,' Michael Poole replied to Jack's question when he took the call on his mobile. 'She rang me several times to say that Sally was drinking, the place was dirty and that Beth wasn't being fed properly.'

'Did you have any proof of this?'

'None whatsoever. That's why I asked social services to look into it, discreetly, if it was possible. They were satisfied that nothing was amiss, so it was left at that. I was surprised that Carol had rung me.'

Knowing what he did, Jack wondered if, at the time, Carol had had a change of heart and wanted Beth to be with her father or else she believed she might talk social services into letting Beth live with her. For Poole was indeed the father even if he believed the wrong woman to be his daughter's mother. Maybe it went deeper than that, maybe Carol envisaged living with Poole and Beth. Whatever was going on it was clear that the sisters were dysfunctional. But then, who isn't even if it's in a small way, Jack asked himself.

Every alibi was now being treble checked. Alice Jones had been serving in her shop all day. A girl who occasionally came in to help had sworn that she had not worked for Alice that day because she spent Tuesdays and Thursdays at college. Poole's whereabouts had been vouched for by several people.

Pressure from above was increasing and Jack did not know how it was possible to have so few leads. No leads, he amended. And if it hadn't been for Rose the true history of the family would not have come to light.

Where was she now? Out working? He glanced out of the window. No, it was far too wet for that.

He paced his office floor, desperate for new ideas. Men and women who had watched the lifeboat rescue the yacht and its crew were still being sought and questioned. Rose had misled them but another potential witness might be found.

'Oh, damn it all,' he said, loudly enough for the head of a passing officer to appear in the doorway. 'It's okay, just thinking aloud,' he muttered. He had been going over and over it; the scene was fixed firmly in his mind; the rainswept beach, the small crowd gathered to watch what might have turned out to be a disaster, the mother with the child she wasn't watching properly because the drama at sea was too compelling and an opportunist making off with Beth. This was initially backed by Rose's statement, but that child had not been Beth.

And suddenly he had seen it clearly. Beth was never on that beach. Only one person could have murdered her and it could not have been more premeditated, and that person was Sally, the woman she had believed to be her mother, the woman she would have trusted when she had been given a drink which contained barbiturates. Sally Jones had killed her, then, either cold-bloodedly or in a state of shock and confusion, had wandered down to the beach. And what an opportunity that sea rescue had given her. No one would have noticed whether or not she had a child with her; all eyes were seaward. When she saw a man walk off with a little girl who resembled Beth, she gave it a minute or two then made the most of it. Sally Jones probably couldn't believe her luck when Rose came forward to confirm her story.

Within seconds two patrol cars were heading towards Marazion. Jack had left minutes before the phone call from Norma Penhalligon came in but its contents were relayed to him as they drove. 'Get an ambulance there, too,' he said.

When they reached the house Norma was waiting with the door open so not a second was wasted. 'I don't know who's with her,' she had said. 'I was out when the visitor arrived but there's an awful lot of shouting and screaming and Sally's threatening to kill someone.'

Jack knew by the way in which the muscles in his neck tightened, that that someone would be Rose. Not again, he prayed, don't let this be happening again.

* * *

Rose watched in horror as Sally drew the blade of the knife across her throat. Her wrists, she thought, I imagined she'd go for her wrists. She was sure she had heard it was impossible to cut your own throat, that the action could not be carried through. Sally had done a good job. There was blood everywhere although her arm had dropped to her side and the knife fell to the floor. Sally staggered; her eyes were wild. Rose, transfixed to the spot, was unable to catch her before she fell. Suddenly she was able to move again. She swiftly grabbed a towel and pressed it tightly to the wound, praying she was doing the right thing. Her phone was in her bag, the bag in the front room. Help was needed urgently but she was afraid that if she released the pressure Sally would bleed to death. Her eyelids were closed and faintly fluttering. Help would not arrive unless she summoned it.

She fled to the front room and picked up Sally's phone, leaving bloodstains on the receiver. She dialled triple nine and gave her name and Sally's address.

She returned to the kitchen. The flow of blood was less strong, she wasn't sure if this was good or bad. The police and an ambulance were already on their way; someone, somehow, had rung for help before her. There was loud knocking on the door. Rose ran to answer it.

Norma, as promised, had waited at the open door. Several pairs of feet thudded up the stairs. Seconds later an ambulance drew up outside and she knew that what she feared had happened. For the past few days Sally had been acting strangely. She went inside and closed her door. The news would arrive in time, it was better to wait for it if it was bad.

Jack surveyed the scene. For agonising seconds all he saw was the blood on Rose. Her face was ashen. An officer took over and Jack helped her to her feet. Her legs buckled so he lowered her into a chair and gently pushed her head down. 'Some deep breaths,' he advised.

'Paramedics,' she heard someone say through the buzzing that filled her ears, but she was determined not to faint. In no time Sally's wound had been dressed and she was strapped to a stretcher.

'Rose?'

She looked up at Jack and tears filled her eyes. Shock, or delayed reaction to the fear she had felt, she supposed, because the tears were not for Sally who had killed the child she loved. Rose was now certain she had done so.

'Can one of you make some tea, please?'

Cupboards were opened and the kettle boiled. Jack dismissed all the officers but one; he could not afford to be alone with this witness, not just because he knew her but because there was the possibility she could be considered as a suspect. There was only her say so that Sally had cut her own throat. The Scenes of Crime team were on their way. 'Did you touch the knife?' he asked once she had a mug of very sweet black tea in front of her.

Rose shook her head. 'I don't know. I don't think so.' It still lay on the floor waiting to be placed in an evidence bag. 'Will she die?'

'It's hard to say. Blood always looks more than it actually is.' But the paramedics had been satisfied that she was still breathing and had a pulse. Hospitals were reluctant to accept patients who were dead on arrival. 'What happened, can you tell me?'

Rose picked up her mug with both hands, oblivious now to the blood. After a couple of sips she explained, as best she could, the events of the morning. 'She was very drunk, Jack. I think she'd already made up her mind to kill herself before I arrived. She knew about Michael and Carol, that's probably what sent her over the top. I also think she might've killed Beth.'

Jack nodded but said nothing about his own suspicions. Like Rose, he wondered how and when she had found out. If Sally died they might never know, nor might they be able to prove she had killed Beth. All they had was circumstantial evidence and even that was shaky – certainly not enough for the DPP to allow it to go to court.

'Let's get you home.' Rose was shivering, shock was setting in. He helped her downstairs and, once in the car, he turned the heater on full. Rose sat in the back with DC Mandy Connors beside her.

'I'll go in with her,' Jack said when they reached the house. 'Radio the station and let me know immediately if there's any news from the hospital. Also, get someone to inform the relatives.'

Inside, Jack made more tea and added a shot of brandy. Rose had been silent on the journey home but she would have been reliving the threat and the eventual outcome. 'I'm not going to leave you on your own. I'll ring Laura. If she's not available then I'm sure Barry will come over.'

Rose nodded; she was in no fit state to argue. 'Jack, Carol found out that Michael was Beth's father.'

'Okay, we'll bear that in mind.' He had to get

back to Camborne, later he would talk to Rose properly. A few minutes later, satisfied that Laura was on her way, Jack left.

The rain was beginning to ease and small patches of blue appeared in the sky as Laura bounded up the drive. She had thrown on a loudly checked jacket of Trevor's which was soaked across the shoulders, as was her hair. 'Oh, my God,' she said, taking in Rose's bloodstained clothes. 'Are you hurt?'

'No. Just shaken.'

'You need a brandy.'

'I've just had one.'

'Then you need another. I certainly do.' Laura took two glasses from the cupboard and reached for the bottle. 'Do you want to talk? If not, I'll just keep my big mouth shut.'

'What I really want is a shower and a change of clothes.'

'That's fine, but I'm coming with you. You don't look as if you can stand, let alone walk.'

Rose was grateful for her assistance and felt a lot better once she was warmly dressed in clean clothes.

Laura lit the fire and sat and listened as Rose went through it all again.

'I really don't believe you at times. How on

earth do you manage to get into these scrapes?'
She sighed. Rose was never going to change. The
unfortunate part was that when she tried to help
people she only succeeded in getting into trouble.
'Look, you can't be alone. Why don't we go to
my place and I'll cook us something. Trevor's at
sea so you won't have to worry about him.'

'Oh, God, I forgot, I've got my class tonight.'

'No way are you taking it. Give me the
numbers and I'll ring around.'

'They're in the file in the drawer in the
kitchen.' Rose was relieved, the last thing she felt
like doing was teaching.

Laura made the necessary calls, explaining that
Rose was ill, then she rang for a taxi. 'It's all settled.
Get your coat, the cab'll be here in five minutes.'

Once she had eaten some colour returned to
Rose's face and Laura was satisfied she would
recover. However, she insisted that she stayed the
night.

CHAPTER FOURTEEN

A tired surgeon had told the police that Sally Jones would live, although she would be badly scarred, but it would be a day or so until she was fit to be questioned. Despite the hospital's reassurance that she would be nursed on a one to one basis because of the suicide attempt, Jack had insisted that an officer remained at her bedside the whole time. It was Friday afternoon before the consultant agreed that the police could now speak to his patient.

Rose knew that the quickest way to get over what she had witnessed was to return to her normal routine as quickly as possible. She spent the rest of the week quietly, working when she felt like it and relaxing in between. On Sunday she and Arthur had driven over to Falmouth then gone on to have lunch in a pub on the Helford Passage. By the following Wednesday she felt almost back to normal, although she had done very little preparation for it. Tonight, she decided, she would give her pupils a bit of fun. She would take along all sorts of things with which to paint; twigs, a dish mop and anything else she could think of. She had known an artist who could produce interesting abstracts by such methods. By the end of the morning she was fully prepared.

The grass was still damp but the driveway had dried overnight. Rose decided that the weather was being kind to her. Once more the sky was a perfect arc of blue and the surface of the sea was ruffled by only tiny waves. She checked her tide table. Conditions were ideal. She would start a painting she had planned in her mind for quite a long time. It was the colours that were important as much as the scene; the golden sands of Hayle, the sea and the golf course in the distance. She filled her flask and set off.

The surface of the sand was dry but underneath it would be damp. Rose spread her waterproof sheet, sat down and got to work. The evenings were pulling in further so only a couple of hours of work were possible. She packed up and went back to the car.

As she drove past Doreen's house she saw her in the small front garden oiling the hinges on the gate. Doreen had recognised the car and waved to her to stop. 'Can you come in for a minute?'

'Yes, but not for long, I've got my class tonight.' Rose parked the car and got out.

'It's just that Katy's here. Sue asked me to look after her while she's at the hospital.'

'What's wrong with her?'

Doreen smiled as they walked around to the kitchen entrance. 'She's pregnant, she's gone to have a scan.'

Katy Overton sat at the kitchen table with a biscuit in her hand and a glass of orange juice in front of her. Her face was solemn. 'This is my friend, Rose,' Doreen said.

'Hello, Katy.' Rose sat down. She knew she would not be able to leave until she had drunk a mug of Doreen's strongly brewed tea. Cyril was nowhere in sight. 'Hello,' the girl replied shyly.

'Did you have a good day in school?' The question brought a frown to her face.

'I don't like school.'

'Oh?' Rose had seen the look of surprise on Doreen's face. 'Why not?'

'I'm not allowed to say.'

'Has a teacher told you that?'

She shook her head and tears filled her eyes. 'A girl.' Katy began crying in earnest.

Rose put an arm around her shoulders and held her close. 'Katy, I think you should say. If you tell us we won't tell anyone else unless we think we ought to.'

'What she said was true. She said she'd kill my mum if I told. And now she's at the hospital.'

Rose was confused. 'Doesn't she know?' she mouthed at Doreen, who shook her head.

'They were going to tell her tonight once they knew the scan was okay.'

'Can you tell me what the problem is, Katy?'

'It's Sarah. She makes me give her my sweets and money. She's seven and bigger than me. She hits me if I don't and she said that about Mum.'

So that's it, Rose thought with relief. Bullying was not pleasant but it could be stopped and it was certainly not as bad as child abuse.

'My goodness, that was easily solved, maid,' Doreen said in admiration. 'I'll let your mummy know when she gets back and she can talk to your teacher. Sarah won't hurt you again, Katy.'

Even Rose was astonished that the child had confided in her so readily but if she didn't know the reason for Sue's hospital visit she must have believed the worst, that her mother was dying, and had been terrified enough to have to tell someone.

'Sue and Simon will be so pleased,' Doreen said as she showed her out. 'That poor chiel's been worried for far too long. Oh, my.' She put her hand to her mouth. 'Did you mention this to Jack?'

'Yes. He sent a PC to the school but I don't know what else he might've done.'

'Then you'd best tell him, maid. We don't want any more upsets. Thank goodness it isn't as bad as I feared. Sue will sort it out now.'

Rose left. She was as astonished as Doreen at the simple outcome to the problem. She went home and changed out of jeans as she usually made an effort to dress more smartly for her pupils.

The class went well; everyone was pleased to be back after the enforced fortnight's holiday, firstly because the roof was being repaired then because of Rose's 'illness'. There were some surprisingly good efforts and a lot of imagination displayed that evening.

The next two days were quiet and the weather held. Rose had finished the mine scene and been back to Hayle to do a bit more work on that oil – and she had finally made the Christmas cake. She was deciding how to spend Friday evening when Jack arrived unexpectedly. He grinned as he kissed her. He's so very handsome, she thought as she took in his tall, lean body, black hair and blue eyes.

'I've come to buy you a celebratory drink. Where shall it be? I don't have the car, though.'

They decided to walk along to the Mount's Bay Inn which was halfway along the Promenade. The stove had been lit and gave off welcome heat. Jack bought their drinks and they sat at a table rather than at their usual places at the bar because he didn't want the conversation to be overheard. 'She's made a full confession,' he said. 'We've also discovered she's had psychiatric treatment several times in the past. She's always been insanely jealous of Carol but she did genuinely love Beth.'

'But she killed her.'

'Yes. And how she regrets it.'

'How did she find out about Michael being Beth's father?'

'She thought there was a vague resemblance but put it down to imagination. However, the day before she killed Beth, Carol mentioned the antique chest their mother had been storing. She recalled that Michael had delivered it and worked out that it was about that time that Carol became pregnant. She rang her mother and demanded to know the truth. Alice Jones, imagining events were far enough in the past for them not to matter, told her. It was the final slap in the face. As we thought, she wanted to hurt them both but she took her hatred out on Beth.'

'Where did the sleeping tablets come from?'

'From a friend. She asked for a few just to tide her over. She won't name the friend, but that's hardly relevant. She claims Beth was unconscious when she smothered her and that ties in with the pathologist's report. We can be thankful for that, at least. Sally is now undergoing psychiatric assessment. Anyway, here's to the end of the case.'

Rose raised her glass in response. 'There's something else you need to know.' She explained what had been troubling Katy. 'And Norma rang to say how wrong she had been about the two sisters.'

Jack was silent for several minutes. He was thinking about Poole and how he had been sure he was lying. It transpired that he wasn't although he had come close to guessing the truth about Beth's parentage when he witnessed the argument. It was that which he had been withholding. 'It's good news about Katy,' he said. 'And now for some more good news. Tomorrow night we're having a proper celebration. Dinner for seven at the Queen's Hotel.'

'Seven?'

'Yes. Us, Laura and Trevor, if they haven't had a row, Barry and Jenny and Arthur.'

Rose leant over and kissed his cheek. 'Thank you,' she said. It was typical of Jack to think of including Arthur.

'And dinner tonight?'

'I haven't thought about it yet.'

'Then why don't I walk you home? We can pick up a Chinese in Newlyn and eat it at your place.'

Rose smiled. She hoped she knew what that would lead to.

ALSO BY JANIE BOLITHO

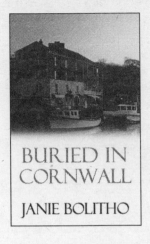

'Trevelyan is clearly set to be the new Miss Marple.'
The Scotsman

'Bolitho is extremely good at plotting . . . this will
take you back to the era of Agatha Christie'
Shots Magazine

'Emotional and involving, truly reflecting Janie's
passion for her home county'
The Cornishman

To discover more great fiction and to
place an order visit our website at
www.allisonandbusby.com
or call us on
020 7580 1080